Murder Most Fowl— Texas Style

Center Point
Large Print

Also by James J. Griffin and available from
Center Point Large Print:

Blood Ties
Death Rides the Rails
Death Stalks the Rangers
Fight for Freedom
The Ghost Riders
Ranger's Revenge
Renegade Ranger
Texas Jeopardy
Tough Month for a Ranger

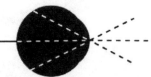

**This Large Print Book carries the
Seal of Approval of N.A.V.H.**

Murder Most Fowl— Texas Style

A Texas Ranger James C. Blawcyzk Novel

James J. Griffin

CENTER POINT LARGE PRINT
THORNDIKE, MAINE

This Center Point Large Print edition
is published in the year 2020 by
arrangement with the author.

This is a work of fiction. The characters, incidents,
and dialogues are products of the author's imagination
and are not to be construed as real.

The text of this Large Print edition is unabridged.
In other aspects, this book may vary
from the original edition.
Printed in the United States of America
on permanent paper.
Set in 16-point Times New Roman type.

ISBN: 978-1-64358-730-1

The Library of Congress has cataloged this record
under Library of Congress Control Number: 2020943873

Murder Most Fowl— Texas Style

Thanks to Jim Huggins, Texas Ranger Sergeant Company A, Retired, and Lecturer of Forensics Science at Baylor University for his invaluable assistance.

Thanks to Texas Ranger Bruce Sherman of Company B for his invaluable assistance.

Thanks to Karl Rehn and Penny Riggs of KR Training in Manheim, Texas for their assistance with firearms information.

For Michele and Eileen

1

The door to the chicken coop swung open, bathing its interior with rays of early morning sunlight.

"Good morning, ladies. Isn't it a lovely day?" the person who'd opened the door said to the hens, as he tossed feed on the coop's dirt floor. "Who wants to be the first lucky lady to begin our new project?"

Most of the hens jumped off their perches and out of their nest boxes to peck at the feed, cackling as they ate. One or two paused, cocked their heads, and looked at their owner. One of these was a Rhode Island Red, large and plump.

"Ah, Camilla, yes. You are the perfect choice. Thank you. Come with me, my dear."

Camilla was scooped up and tucked under her owner's left arm. She pecked at the corn he held in his right hand, while he crossed the pen and latched its gate. Whistling, he stroked her head as he walked across the yard, then placed her in a crate in the back of his truck. Once certain the hen was secured, he got in the truck, started it, and drove off.

2

Kimberly Blawcyzk had just finished her morning shower and gotten dressed for the day. She walked back into the bedroom to find her husband, Texas Ranger James Blawcyzk, still in bed, lying on his belly, sound asleep. Ordinarily, he was up and out of the house well before her.

"Jim, it's high time you got up," she said. "I've already had my shower and gotten dressed."

Jim didn't move.

"Jim, did you hear me? Wake up."

"Mmnpfh."

Jim burrowed his face more deeply into his pillow. Kim pulled the sheet off him.

"Jim, get up!"

Jim lifted his head to look at her, bleary-eyed.

"Kim, darlin', listen to me. For the first time in months, I've got all my work cleaned up. I don't have one single case hangin' over my head. So I've got nothin' to do this weekend, nothin' at all. Plus, on Monday I have to start coverin' Llano County for the next twelve weeks, while Stacy Martinez is on maternity leave. As if I don't have enough to do with the four counties I've already got. All of which means I'm stayin' right here in this bed the entire weekend. I just might not even go to church tomorrow."

He buried his face back in his pillow. Kim glared at him in exasperation, then took the waistband of his briefs, stretched it as far as the elastic would go, and let it snap back against Jim's butt.

"Ow! What'd you go and do that for?" Jim grumbled.

"To get you up. You can't just lie around all day. You promised to assemble the chicken coop for me and your mother today, remember? You also said you'd watch Josh. We're going to pick up the chicks and feed this afternoon, after we do the grocery shopping, then stop by to visit with the Crandalls. And don't forget, I've invited the new neighbors over for dinner tomorrow evening."

"I've already got two goldang mother hens around here," Jim mumbled. "I sure don't need any more."

"What did you just say, Jim?"

"Nothin'. That was me snoring."

"Don't try and give me that. Now, are you getting out of that bed, or not?"

"Not."

"I'm warning you. Don't make me turn into a Washington, D.C. politician, and force me to use the nuclear option."

"Not even a bomb will get me off this mattress,"

Jim answered. He took his pillow and covered his head with it.

"All right. You asked for it, cowboy."

Kim took their ten-month-old son, Josh, from his playpen and sat him atop his father.

"Frostie!" she called. It took less than a minute for the family's light tan, Wheaten/Cairn terrier cross to come bounding into the room, carrying one of his squeaky doggie pacifiers. He dropped it at Kim's feet, then stood looking at her expectantly, tongue lolling and tail wagging.

"Do you want me to hide your toy, Frostie?"

Kim picked up the toy and shoved it under Jim's pillow. Frostie immediately jumped on the bed and burrowed under the pillow, pawing at Jim as he searched for the pacifier. He dug it out, then perched his two front feet on Jim's back, happily shoving the toy against Jim's neck and squeaking it wildly, shaking his head and growling. Josh was bouncing on his father's back, giggling.

"Frostie, go!" Jim snatched the toy and threw it across the room. Frostie chased after it, grabbed it and raced down the hallway. Josh started pulling his father's hair.

"All right, all right. You win, Kim. I'm getting up."

Jim rolled onto his back, and lifted Josh into the air.

"How ya doin', little pard? Soon as I throw some clothes on, you want to come with me while I feed the horses? Then we'll come back in and have some breakfast."

"Aren't you going to shower before you eat?" Kim asked.

Jim shook his head.

"Uh-uh. Nope. It ain't worth botherin' to clean up. After I feed the horses, then eat, I've got to muck out the stalls and corral, then start to work on your danged chicken coop. I'll be all dirty and sweaty ten minutes after I begin. Those hens had better lay a lot of eggs once they're old enough, or they'll be mighty tasty for supper."

"I'm more worried about Frostie thinking they're his dinner, on the hoof, as it were."

"He'll be fine with 'em, since they'll be kept behind a fence, with mesh over it so they can't fly out," Jim answered. "You need to be more worried about raccoons, coyotes, or foxes sneakin' around at night, gettin' under the fence, and snatchin' those chicks. Might even have some snakes slither into the coop to suck down some of the eggs. I reckon I'll dig a trench about a foot deep to place the fence in. Most critters won't dig that far down."

"Thanks, honey. I love you, you know that?"

"Only for my terrific body and handsome face," Jim retorted, with a grin. "I'm just a boy toy for you."

"Actually, it's the hat, belt buckle, and boots," Kim shot back.

"Oh, a cowboy toy. Glad we got *that* straightened out," Jim answered. "C'mon, Josh, let's get goin'."

Jim sat up, then placed Josh on the floor. He threw on a faded pair of jeans, pulled on a pair of socks and his boots, then tugged a Yellowstone National Park T-shirt over his head. Lastly, he donned a Texas Rangers Company F baseball cap.

"Anythin' you need before I head outside, Kim?"

"Not that I can think of."

"Good. Okay, Josh, here we go."

He lifted the baby and sat him on his shoulders, then called the dog.

"C'mon, Frostie. Time for you to chase any varmints you find outta the barn . . . and I don't mean the cats. You leave them alone. Kim, pick up some nice big T-bones, and I'll grill 'em for supper tonight. Tell George and Emma I said howdy."

"I'll do that. You have a good day. Love you," Kim answered.

"You and Ma have fun today," he replied, then kissed Kim on the cheek.

"You too, Jim," she said.

Kim returned his kiss with one to his lips, along with running her fingertips lightly down his chest.

"If you're not too tired tonight, I'll thank you properly for putting that coop together, once your mother goes home."

16

"Promise?"

"Promise."

"Then I'm not tired one bit."

"That's what I thought."

"Where's that darn dog? *Frostie!*" Jim called again.

Frostie ran into the bedroom.

"All right, you two. Time to get to work."

With Josh on his shoulders, and Frostie tagging along behind, Jim headed for the barn.

Jim was relaxing on the back patio, drinking a beer, with Frostie and Josh playing alongside him. Frostie was doing the "downward dog", his chin on the ground between his front feet and his rump in the air, tail wagging, barking at Josh. The baby was batting at Frostie's front paws. Every time he made contact, the dog would jump back, bark even louder, then charge at Josh once again.

"You two sure have a lot more energy left than I do," Jim said. "Looks like playtime's about over, though. Here comes your mom and grandma."

Kim braked her Chevy Equinox to a stop at the end of the driveway. Jim's mother, Betty, rolled down her window.

"Jim, we've got the chicks. Come help us get them into the coop."

"All right, I'll meet you back there," Jim answered. To Josh, he continued. "C'mon, little pard, let's go see these birds your mom and grandma are so all-fired excited about. Frostie, you'd better come too, so you'll learn they're not your new chew toys, or worse, your supper."

Carrying Josh, Jim walked over to the chicken coop, which was between the house and the horse barn. Kim had already opened the lift gate of her SUV, and the gate to the chicken pen. She and Betty were removing several cardboard carriers filled with peeping chicks. Frostie sniffed at the boxes, curious as to their contents.

"How many of those things did you buy?" Jim asked.

"An even dozen," Kim answered. "Jim, you did a wonderful job building the coop. It looks perfect."

"I didn't do all that much, since it was a kit. All I had to do was put the pieces together, then nail them in place."

"You still did a good job," Betty said. "Would you mind opening the door, so we can get these little peeps inside?"

"They're marshmallow?"

"No, they are *not* marshmallow, Jim, you goof," Kim answered. "But if you make any more jokes like that about our chickens I'll smash the first egg that's laid over your head."

"Isn't raw egg supposed to be good for your hair?"

"Jim, just open the door."

"All right, all right. Frostie, you stay out here."

Once Jim opened the door to the coop, Betty and Kim carried the chicks inside. They placed the boxes on the floor, opened them, and waited for the chicks to come out and explore their new home. Two chicks tentatively stuck their heads out, then hopped from their box onto the floor. The rest quickly followed.

"What in the world kind of chickens did you two buy?" Jim asked. "I've never seen chicks like these. There's not a fuzzy yellow one in the whole bunch. Plus, some of them look like they have powder puffs on their heads."

"Flock," Betty corrected.

"Ma! Your language!"

"I said 'flock', Jim. Chickens come in flocks, not a bunch, nor herds like horses or cows."

"The gray and white ones are Ameraucanas," Kim explained. "Their feathers will be a pretty silver-white color once they've come in. They also lay pale blue or blue-green eggs, so we can have Easter eggs all year 'round. The ones with the powder puffs, as you call them, are golden-laced, silver-laced, and splash Polish chickens. We bought those because they look so comical, and, well, because they're Polish, like you."

"If I ever grow a head of hair like that, I'll need a new barber. What do you think, Josh?"

Jim scooped up one of the chicks and held it for Josh to touch. When Josh reached out and

19

touched the chick, it pecked at his hand. Josh giggled.

"I guess you like 'em, huh, little pard?"

"Jim, put that poor thing down," Kim told him. "They're not pets."

"Oh, but they soon will be, if I know you two," Jim retorted, as he lowered his hand so the chick could flutter to the floor and join the rest of the flock, which were busily pecking at the feed in their tray.

"Oh, like you don't spoil your animals, Jim," Betty said.

"I don't, not one bit. I didn't give Frostie one of these chicks to play with, did I?"

"And you'd better not," Kim answered. "You still haven't said what you think of them."

"They're kinda cute," Jim answered. "And as long as they give me fresh eggs for breakfast, that's all that really matters—leastwise, far as I'm concerned."

"They will, once they're a little older," Kim assured him. "Did you connect the heat lamp? They need that, so they don't get a chill, catch pneumonia, and die."

"It's all set," Jim answered. "Although why these things would need a heat lamp in the middle of a Texas summer is beyond me."

"They only need it until they've grown some," Betty answered. "And on cool, damp days. We should probably leave them alone for a while and let them get used to their new home. We can check on them in an hour or so."

"Speaking of eating . . ." Jim began.

"Betty, we weren't speaking of eating, were we?"

"Kim, you should know by now, Jim is almost *always* speaking of eating, or at least thinking about it," Betty answered.

"Yes, so speaking of eating, did you get the steaks, Kim?"

"I did. And a big beef knuckle for Frostie. That should keep him distracted, and away from the chicks."

"He'll learn they're not for him, soon enough," Jim said. "I'll meet you and Ma back at the house. I'm gonna fire up the grill. I've got some mesquite logs that'll add some real nice flavor to the steaks. I'll roast some corn and potatoes, too. C'mon, Josh, let's get supper goin'. You and Frostie can give me a hand while your mom and grandma finish playin' with the chickens."

Jim shook his head.

"Boy, howdy, I sure never did expect to see the day when my own wife and mother gave me the bird."

"Jim, out! Now!" Kim ordered. "Or I'll feed the banana cream pie I bought you to the chicks."

"You wouldn't."

"Just try me."

"I'm not takin' that chance," Jim said. "Time to get cookin'."

• • •

Late that night, Jim and his wife were lying in bed. Kim had already fallen asleep, with her head on his chest. A slight smile played across his face.

Boy howdy, I'm the danged luckiest hombre in Texas. I've got a job I love, a nice home, and my family's all here with me. Ma's got her little place behind ours, so she's not all that lonesome after Pa got himself killed.

Jim was a sixth-generation Texas Ranger, a descendant of the original James Blawcyzk, who had been a Ranger in the 1870s. Just like the first Jim Blawcyzk, his father had been killed in the line of duty, while foiling a terrorist plot to blow up the Alamo. Jim's property had been in the family since his ancestor purchased it, and built a homestead. After his father died, Jim's mother nearly lost the land to a pair of corrupt county commissioners. Those men were now in prison, and Jim had made certain the land would never be out of Blawcyzk ownership again. If the family died out, the acreage would become a county park.

Kim shifted slightly, her head still on Jim's chest, but her hand now lying on his stomach. Jim sighed, thinking about the lovemaking session he and Kim had finished earlier.

It was a pure stroke of luck the day I met Kim, too. She's pretty, smart . . . in fact, a helluva lot smarter'n I am—and puts up with me, not to mention my bein' a Ranger, which keeps me away at all hours. I still thank the Good Lord for her, and Josh. Plus, with any luck, after tonight, Josh just might have a little sister or brother nine months down the road.

Jim had met Kimberly Maria Tavares when she literally ran into him, while rushing to meet a filing deadline at the Kendall County Courthouse, where Jim had just testified at a trial. He asked her to supper, surprised when she accepted. Over their meal, he found out her family had been in Texas since it was still part of Mexico. She owned her own firm, Tavares Consulting, which assisted minority and women owned start-up businesses, and also helped companies wishing to do business in Mexico navigate the regulations and red tape. She and Jim were both tall, she being five-foot-eight, he standing six-foot-four in his stocking feet, but that was where the resemblance ended. Kim was dark-skinned, with raven black hair and eyes, and a slim, but nicely curved, figure. Jim was so fair his pale skin never tanned, only burned, his hair was blonde, and his eyes a deep, crystalline blue. While Kim wasn't a cover model beauty, and Jim was ruggedly good-looking, but certainly not movie star handsome, they did make a striking couple.

Now if only I could get a few more days before the bad guys start actin' up again.

With that thought, Jim drifted off to sleep.

3

"Kim, I'll see you tonight. You and Ma have a good day," Jim said. He was standing at the open back door. "Unless somethin' comes up, I'll be in my office all day, getting caught up on some old paperwork. What've you got planned?"

"I've got a meeting with some potential new clients this morning. After that, just the usual," Kim answered.

"Sounds like we both might have an easy day, for once," Jim said. Just then, his cell phone rang.

"I hope you didn't just jinx us," Kim said, as Jim fished the phone out of its holster on his belt.

"Ranger Blawcyzk."

"Ranger Blawcyzk, Dispatch. We have a request for assistance from the Llano County Sheriff's Office. Apparent homicide."

"What's the location?"

"10229 Nixon Road, which is also County 408. Site is approximately twelve miles east of Valley Spring."

"Got it. On my way. ETA sixty to seventy-five minutes."

"Will notify Llano you are en route."

"Obliged."

"You *did* just jinx us, didn't you?" Kim said, once Jim hung up.

"Yep. Well, me, anyway. Looks like I've got a murder way up in Llano County. What a way to start the week. Gotta run."

Jim gave Kim a quick kiss, then went out to his dark blue Chevy Tahoe. He fired up the engine, switched on the red and blue strobe lights hidden behind the grille, threw the big SUV in gear, and roared out of the driveway.

Just over eighty minutes later, Jim rolled up to the address he'd been given. A rainbow flag fluttered from atop a hand lettered sign which read: *Free Range, Organic Chicken Available. Also Eggs from Free Range Hens. No Antibiotics, Steroids, or GMOs. Hatched and Raised Right Here at Those Two Gals From Llano Chicken Farm.*

"Oh, Lord, I sure hope this isn't gonna turn out to be a hate crime," Jim muttered, when he saw the flag. He pulled to a stop in front of the yellow crime scene tape stretched across the driveway and lowered his window. The Llano County deputy securing the entrance got out of his Dodge Charger. Apparently, word had not yet leaked to the news media, for there were no television reporters or satellite trucks in sight.

"Howdy, Deputy," Jim said. "Ranger James Blawcyzk, out of Buda. I'm coverin' for Ranger Martinez."

"Howdy, Ranger," the deputy answered. "The house is about a quarter-mile up this dirt road, around the bend. Sheriff Avery is waitin' for you. I'll take down the tape."

"Obliged."

Once the deputy lowered the tape, Jim drove over it and up to the house, a low brick structure surrounded by well-tended gardens of native plants. A green Ram pickup was in front of a nearby shed, a dark red Subaru Forester was alongside the gardens. Three Llano County Sheriff's Department Ford Explorers were parked out front. County Sheriff Frederick Avery got out of the nearest one. He walked up to Jim and shook his hand.

"Howdy, Jim. It's been a long while. You didn't take all that much time to get here, bein' as you had to drive up all the way from Buda. I'm sure glad Austin has you coverin' for Stacy, not someone I don't know."

"Howdy yourself, Fred. I was still at home, so that saved me a few minutes. What've you got?"

"One victim, Lillian Gates, of this address. Female Caucasian, forty-four years old. Hanging, from what it appears. However, as you'll see in a minute, there's something peculiar about this one. That's why I called in the Rangers. She was found by her partner, in that large shed over yonder. The body's still where she found it."

"Where's the partner?"

"Mary Connors? Inside the house, with one of my deputies. We've already done a preliminary

26

interview, but I told her she'd have to speak with you."

"Sounds like you've got things well in hand, as usual, Fred. Let me get the evidence collection kit from my truck and put my BDU on, then I'll have a look."

"Sure thing."

Jim opened the tailgate of his Tahoe, donned his protective BDU, two pairs of nitrile gloves, and slid two pairs of vinyl booties over his cowboy boots. He took his evidence gathering kit from its place, then slammed the truck's tailgate shut.

"Lead the way, Fred."

Avery took Jim over to the shed and opened the door. The lights were still on, so once he and Jim were inside, he pulled the door shut. In the middle of the shed, hanging from a rafter, was the body of a woman, fully clothed. Her feet were about two feet above the shed's floor. Alongside her hung a dead chicken.

"What the hell?" Jim exclaimed. Then, involuntarily, he laughed.

"You think somethin's funny here, Ranger?" Avery asked, a bit perturbed by Jim's reaction.

"No, not at all, Fred. I apologize for laughin'. I tried not to, but I couldn't keep it in. Y'see, my wife and mother decided they just *had* to have a flock of hens. I spent almost my entire day Saturday buildin' a damn coop for the chicks they brought home. Now, the first case I'm facin' after

27

that involves someone who hung a chicken. Just struck me funny. It's outta my system, now. Let's get to work."

Jim took out his camera and digital recorder. He switched both on, spoke his name, the date, time, and case number into the recorder, then began dictating his observations as he took pictures of the corpse, and the dead chicken, from all angles.

"With me is Llano County Sheriff Frederick Avery. Victim is a white female. Per Sheriff Avery, she is Lillian Gates, of 10229 Nixon Road, Llano County, Texas, this address. Her body was discovered by Mary Connors, also of this address, at approximately eight A.M. this date. Victim was found hanging from a rafter in a large shed on the property. Also hanging from the same rafter is a good-sized red hen. Preliminary examination of the scene would indicate homicide, not suicide. There is no object near the body which the victim might have used for support while she tied the apparent murder weapon around her neck, nor any object which might have been used by the victim to reach the rafter, then kicked away. There has also been no suicide note found, as of yet. However, there is no sign of forced entry, nor a struggle, leaving suicide still a possibility. Death appears to have occurred within the last few hours. Once the victim's body is lowered, I will examine it further, to narrow the time of death, and also make a more positive determination as to whether Ms. Gates was a homicide victim, or died by her own hand. Once I have completed my examination, the body will be turned over to the Llano County Coroner for a complete autopsy."

Jim switched off the recorder.

"Fred, would you bring in a couple of your deputies to help take this poor woman down? I'll do some quick lookin' around in here while you go for them."

"Sure thing, Jim. I'll have 'em right here."

While he waited for Avery to return, Jim did a preliminary search of the garage, looking for anything obviously out of place, or any clues the perpetrator might have left, intentionally or otherwise. The only item he found, directly below the corpse, was a long, brunette hair. He used a pair of tweezers to lift that from the floor and placed it in a baggie, to be examined further, after he questioned Mary Connors. After that, he took a stepladder, which was leaning against the back wall of the shed, dusted it for finger or hand prints, then used it to climb up alongside the corpse, so he could examine the rafter from whic the victim hung. He took more photographs, including some close ups of the rope and knot. Finally, he untied the dead chicken. He'd just come back down the ladder and sealed the chicken in a large plastic bag when Avery returned, along with two deputies.

"Jim, these are deputies Angela Martin and Josh Dubois. I've already explained to them you're covering for Ranger Martinez."

"Appreciate your help, deputies," Jim said. "What I need you to do is lift the victim just enough to put some slack in the rope, so I can untie it. Once that's done, I'll help you lower her to the floor. We'll need to lay her on her back, okay?"

Both deputies nodded. Jim ascended the ladder again.

"I'm ready."

The deputies wrapped their arms around the corpse's legs, lifting it just high enough to take pressure off the rope. Jim had to use the point of his pocketknife to start unraveling the knot, then untied it.

"Go ahead, take her down. Slow and easy. Fred, if you could grab her shoulders once she's low enough, I'd appreciate it. I want to take some samples from this beam, and a few more pictures."

"Sure thing, Jim. You've got it."

With the deputies supporting the body, Jim used the rope to gently drop it until Avery could take its shoulders. Once it was in Avery's grasp, Jim let loose of the rope, and turned his attention to the rafter. He took more photos, then dusted it for prints. Finally, he used his knife to take several scrapings from the wood, which he placed in another baggie, and sealed that shut. Once done, he descended the ladder, sealed the rope in a large plastic bag, and placed the samples in his evidence case.

"Let's see what we have here," he said. He took more photos of the body, particularly the neck, then switched on his recorder, and hunkered alongside the dead woman.

"I am now performing my examination of the body of Lillian Gates."

Jim slowly turned Gates's head from side to side.

"It appears, which will be confirmed by the autopsy, the victim's neck was not broken, but death was caused by asphyxiation due to strangulation. Bruise patterns on the neck and throat indicate the victim did struggle for breath before succumbing."

He lifted Gates's arms, then her legs, and rolled her jeans up above her ankles, before removing her sneakers.

"Rigor mortis has begun, but has not progressed very far. Livor mortis is also present, but not set. Pooling of the blood and bodily fluids is primarily in the feet and ankles, with a minimal amount in the fingers and hands. This would indicate victim was hung while still alive, rather than being killed elsewhere, then hung. There are also no drag marks which might indicate the body had been pulled across the floor of this shed, before being hung. None of the dust present on surfaces has been disturbed, nor are there any signs of blood, nor scraps of cloth which might indicate victim was strangled before body was hung.

Most importantly, there are no bruises on the victim's neck consistent with strangulation by hand, only rope burns, abrasions, and contusions consistent with hanging. Victim is also fully clothed, most likely ruling out sexual assault. Again, that will be confirmed by the county medical examiner. Based on the condition of the body, estimated time of death is within the past two to six hours."

Jim switched off the recorder.

"Fred, I'm going to question Mary Connors now. I want this shed sealed off until I'm done with that. No one, not even you, is to come back inside this shed until I've had a chance to go through it more thoroughly. I need one of your deputies to guard it until I'm done with Ms. Connors."

"The coroner should be here within half-an-hour. Will he be able to remove the body?"

"No, he's gonna have to wait until I give the okay. When he does get here, I'll want him to remove Ms. Gate's clothing, seal it in plastic bags, and hold it aside for me. With any luck, I'll be able to get some DNA samples off it. Also, don't give the news media any information, except that we're investigating an untimely death, until I say so. The one thing I especially *don't* want the public to know about is the chicken. That's a detail I want kept under wraps. It's somethin' only the perpetrator would know, and I'd like to keep it that way, until I'm ready to release that information to the public."

"Of course, Jim. Martin, Dubois, you heard the Ranger's orders. Remain outside the door to this shed until we return. Don't let anyone near it, and if any damn reporters somehow manage to get past Jones, chase 'em off the property. If they give you an argument, arrest 'em for trespassing, and interfering with a criminal investigation. You understand me?"

"Yes, sir," Dubois said.

"Of course, Sheriff," Martin answered.

"Good. C'mon, Jim," Avery said with a nod, "I'll take you up to the house."

Mary Connors was in her living room, along with another Llano County deputy. She had been weeping, but now sat stoically, wringing the handkerchief in her hands.

Jim introduced himself.

"Ms. Connors, I'm Texas Ranger James Blawcyzk. I'll be taking the lead in the investigation of Ms. Gates's death. First, please accept my condolences on your loss."

"Thank you, Ranger."

"You're welcome. Now, I realize this will be

difficult, and I am aware Sheriff Avery has already interviewed you; however, it's necessary that I also question you. It's imperative to do that right now, so I can obtain as much information as possible about Ms. Gates's final hours, while the events of this morning are still fresh in your memory. If you don't believe you are prepared at this moment, I can speak with you later, but it would be better if I could conduct my interview now."

"That will be fine, Ranger Blawcyzk. I'll manage."

"Thank you. I appreciate your cooperation. If at any time you need to stop, just say so. Do you mind if I record our conversation?"

"No, not at all."

"Will you allow myself and the Llano County officers to search your property without a search warrant? If not, then we'll wait until we obtain one. I'll also need to search your vehicles, perhaps have one or both impounded for further examination."

"I've already sent a deputy to the courthouse to request a warrant, Jim," Avery said.

"That's good, Fred. However, Ms. Connors, it would be helpful to have your permission to start the search before the warrant arrives."

"Of course, Ranger, I understand that, and you have my permission to search our entire property. I also realize it will be necessary for you to go through our vehicles. If it helps, I haven't used the Forester for at least a month. I usually drove the pickup."

"Thank you, Ms. Connors. I trust you have no objection to my recording your permission, for the record?"

"None at all."

"Again, I appreciate your cooperation. If you are ready, I'll start the interview now."

"Certainly. Go ahead."

Jim switched on his recorder.

"I am now proceeding to interview Ms. Mary Connors, the person who found the victim's body. Ma'am, for the record, would you give your full name and address?"

"Mary Ann Louise Connors, 10229 Nixon Road, Llano County, Texas."

"Also, for the record, you have given me your permission to search your entire property, including buildings and vehicles, prior to obtaining a search warrant. You also understand Sheriff Avery is requesting a search warrant, and it is your right to not have your property searched until the aforesaid warrant is obtained, and that, until it is obtained, you have the right to stop the search of your property at any time."

"That is correct."

"Thank you. Before I start my questioning, I have to advise you that, since you are not a suspect in any crime at this moment, I am not required to provide you the rights of an accused person. However, you do have the right to refuse to answer any or all questions, and to stop the questioning at any time. You also have the right to have your attorney present before I begin questioning you, and you have the right to stop the interview until you have legal counsel present. Do you understand these rights?"

"Yes."

"Then I'll proceed. Take all the time you need to answer my questions. You and Ms. Gates both resided at this address, is that correct?"

"Yes."

"Were you and Ms. Gates in a relationship?"

"Yes."

"Exactly what was that relationship?"

"We were married. Lillian was my wife."

"I understand. Were you and Ms. Gates also business partners?"

"That is correct. We ran a small chicken and vegetable farm, offering organic free-range chicken and eggs, along with organic vegetables in season."

"Was your business stable, financially?"

"We were doing quite well, yes."

"Now, as best you can recall, relate everything you did this morning, up until the time you discovered Ms. Gates's body. Take a few moments to gather your thoughts if you need to."

Connors sighed, swallowed hard, then began.

"Lillian and I had ordered a new brand of feed for our birds. It was several days late in being delivered. It finally came in last night. We were nearly out of feed, but had enough to make it until this morning. Frank Jordan, who owns the local feed store, promised to open at seven so we could pick up the feed first thing. When I left the house at six-thirty, everything was fine. Lillian was just waking up, and getting ready to take her shower."

"Mr. Jordan will be able to confirm the approximate time you arrived at his store, and how long you spent there?"

"Yes."

"Before you left, there was no sign of Ms. Gates being upset, or perhaps distressed about something? Had she been depressed lately? Perhaps not acting like her normal self?"

"Not at all. She seemed as happy as always. Lillian had a much more positive outlook than I have. She always managed to cheer me up when I was feeling down."

"There didn't appear to be anyone about the place when you left?"

Connors shook her head.

"Not that I noticed. Of course, I wasn't looking for anyone."

"That's understandable. You don't have a dog that would have given a warning, if a stranger was around?"

"No. We have a few barn cats to keep away the rodents, and two house cats. That's all."

"I see. Please, continue."

"All right. When I returned from Jordan's Feed, I parked in front of the shed, then went inside to look for Lillian. I wanted her to help me unload the truck. She wasn't in the house, so I went out to the chicken coops, thinking she'd gone to gather eggs. When she wasn't there either, I decided to unload the truck myself. When I opened the shed's door, that's when . . ." Connors's voice broke. "That's when I found her."

"She was already dead?"

"Yes, I'm certain of that."

"I need you to think very hard now. Did you notice anything out of place in the shed? Anything at all, no matter how insignificant it might seem?"

Connors thought for a few moments, then shook her head.

"No. The only thing I did notice was some chicken feed spilled on the floor. Lillian would never have left that mess. She would have swept it up."

"That means she apparently died before she had a chance to," Jim said. "This is another important question. Do you have any idea why one of your chickens was hung along with Ms. Gates?"

"One of our chickens? That bird wasn't one of ours."

"Are you certain?"

"Ranger, I'm positive. The only birds we have in our flocks are Hollands, Andalusians, and Speckeldys, which are also known as Speckled Rangers. The hen which was alongside Lillian was a Rhode Island Red. We've never had any of those. That bird belonged to someone else."

"There's no other farm nearby it could have come from?"

"The only nearby neighbors obtain their eggs from us. I don't know of anyone else within five miles who has chickens. And as you probably know, chickens aren't good flyers. Any number of predators would have caught and killed that hen before it could reach here."

"That makes sense, which increases the probability that your wife's death was indeed a homicide. If you are able to continue, I have a few more questions. Or would you rather take a few minutes to rest, and compose yourself?"

"No, I want to get this over with, so whoever killed Lillian is found as soon as possible."

"Thank you. Now, do you know of anyone who would have reason to murder Ms. Gates, or yourself? Anyone who might have had an argument with either of you, or held a grudge? A family member, perhaps?"

"No, Ranger. No one. We both have several nieces and nephews, I have two brothers, Lillian had two sisters and a brother. We all get along fine, and visit often. The kids love to come here, run around, gather eggs, and play with the chickens."

"How long have you and Ms. Gates lived here?"

"About seven years now."

"Have you ever had problems with anyone because of your lifestyle, that is, being lesbian? I apologize if the question offends you in any way, but it has to be asked. I'm trying to determine a motive for the apparent homicide of your wife."

"Not in quite some time, Ranger. For the past several years, in fact. Oh, we still get the occasional good ol' boy or gal who will drive past and shout insults, but nothing serious. We've learned to take that in stride."

"But you did have some trouble at one time?"

"We did, when we first moved out here from Llano. Most folks welcomed us with open arms when we bought this place, but there were a few who didn't want us here. Or, at least, didn't approve. Eventually, once they got to know us, they became friends, or at least tolerated us, and left us alone. In fact, some of the young men who were the most insulting found out we could give as well as they gave. Lillian and I started shouting insults right back at them. Now, it's a standing joke between them and us. They'll come by, purchase some eggs or meat, then say good-bye with an insult, which we give right back. Or they'll be driving by and we'll yell at each other. What started out as, I don't want to say hatred, but dislike, or ignorance, on both sides, has turned into friendships, with plenty of good-natured teasing. Lillian and I are always invited to any of the steer roasts or barbeques in the area. We've been pretty well accepted by our neighbors, and the folks in town."

"I'll still need to speak with those people," Jim said. "Would you mind giving their names to Sheriff Avery?"

"Not at all."

"I'm obliged. For the moment, I don't have any further questions for you, Ms. Connors. I may have once I've finished going over the scene and searching your property. Do you have anything you wish to ask me?"

"I will need to stay here until you say I'm free to leave, correct?"

"That is correct, Ms. Connors. If you do need anything, I'm certain Sheriff Avery would be happy to send one of his deputies for it."

"I sure would, Ms. Connors," Avery said.

"I'm grateful to both of you. The only thing I need right now is to make arrangements for Lillian's . . . funeral."

Connors dabbed at her eyes, as tears began to flow, yet again.

"I'm very sorry, Ms. Connors, but I won't be able to let you know when those can be made, for at least a few days. The county coroner has to perform an autopsy before Ms. Gates's body can be released for burial. I will do everything in my authority to speed up the process as much as possible. However, the autopsy is absolutely crucial to make a final determination as to the cause of Ms. Gates's death, and may well provide key evidence I need to find and arrest her killer. I hope you understand."

"I do. You take as long as you need, and do whatever has to be done, to find the damned son of a bitch who killed my wife."

"You have my word on that," Jim answered. "Fred, if you would have one of your deputies stay with Ms. Connors, I'd like to have your help while I finish up outside. Ms. Connors, you can give the list of people I requested to the deputy. Fred, I also want a roadblock set up in front of the driveway here. I want it kept in place for the next twenty-four hours. I need every motorist passing by stopped and asked if they saw anything out of the ordinary between midnight and eight this morning."

"It'll be done, Jim."

"Good. Ms. Connors, I will be here for quite some time," Jim said. "I've got to make certain I don't miss any evidence the perpetrator might have left behind. If you think of anything which might be helpful in the meantime, have the deputy call Sheriff Avery."

"Of course, Ranger."

"Thank you for your cooperation. Once again, please accept my condolences on your loss."

Jim clicked off his recorder.

"Fred, we'll go back to the shed first, then return to the house."

"Sure doesn't look like whoever did this left much to go on, Jim," Avery said, as they began going through the shed.

"I've picked up a couple of things, but you're right," Jim agreed. "I just want to go through this shed once again, and finish dusting it for prints. After that, I'll go through the vehicles, to see if there's any sign of blood or anything else useful, but I doubt I'll find anything. Same for the fingerprints. I doubt I'll find any but the two women's, at least any clear enough to be usable. My first look tells me whoever hung Ms. Gates didn't use a ladder or somethin' else to hang her from that rafter. It appears whoever it was got the rope around her neck, then tossed it over the beam and pulled her up. Her neck wasn't broken, which it most likely would have been if she'd been stood on, say a stool, which was then kicked out from under her. My guess is the killer was watching her, then followed her into the shed, and took her by complete surprise. If I do find any prints, they'll most likely be on the door, since it was closed when Ms. Connors arrived home. Well, let's get to work. By the way, why are you looking at me kinda funny?"

"I'm just making certain you're not a Speckled Ranger, that's all," Avery answered, laughing. "Never heard of a Texas Ranger bein' a chicken before."

"You want there to be a *second* murder on this farm today, Fred? Yours?"

"No. I'm sorry, Jim. Besides, you've got freckles, not speckles."

"Fred, do me a favor. Just shut up and concentrate on what needs doin'."

"All right. No need to get your cockles up like an angry rooster. Besides, you've got a helluva lot of nerve, complainin' about *my* jokes, considerin' the ones you come up with."

About an hour later, after having examined the shed and its contents, along with the Ram and Subaru, to his satisfaction, and released the body of Lillian Gates to the county coroner, Jim instructed the sheriff to have his deputies search the rest of the farm, except the chicken coops, for any evidence that might be found, while he returned to the house. As Jim had ordered, a deputy was still with Mary Connors.

"Did you find anything which might lead you to Lillian's murderer?" Connors asked, when he came back inside.

"Perhaps. I'll know more, once I get what I did

find to the lab for testing. Now, I would like to ask a favor of you."

"What would that be?"

"I'd appreciate it if you would take me out to the chicken coops. I need you to see if anything is out of place at those."

"Of course."

"I'm obliged. Deputy, you stay in this house. No one else, except Sheriff Avery, is allowed to enter until I return."

"Understood, Ranger."

Connors led Jim outside, around the back of the house, to where several large, airy coops were surrounded and topped by chicken wire.

"Even though the birds we raise are considered cage-free, or free range, it's necessary to keep them penned so predators can't get at them, Ranger," Connors explained.

"That makes sense," Jim agreed. "What I need you to do is take me inside the coops, to see if you notice anything amiss."

"All right."

Connors took Jim through the coops, both of them looking for any sign of intruders.

"There's nothing out of place here, either," Connors said, after they went through the last of the coops. "Like all the others, the nest boxes are in place, the feed trays aren't moved, and there don't seem to be any hens or chicks missing."

"Then I only have one more outbuilding to

45

check," Jim said. "The greenhouse over yonder."

"Is that really necessary, Ranger?"

"I'm afraid it is. Is there something in there you don't want me to see?"

"I guess not."

Connors took Jim over to the small greenhouse.

"I've got to get a key from my pocket to unlock the door," she said.

"All right, go ahead."

Connors removed a key from her jeans' right pocket, unlocked and opened the greenhouse door. One glance inside told Jim why she was reluctant to show him its contents. The building was filled with marijuana plants, most almost ready to be harvested.

"I know, Ranger. It's illegal. Would it help if I told you we only sell this to people who need it for medical reasons?"

"I'm not concerned about what you've got here," Jim answered. "I'll let the sheriff know, and it'll be up to him to decide what action he'll take, if any. I'm here to solve the apparent murder of your wife. These plants do give me a possible motive. Someone may have killed Ms. Gates to get their hands on this marijuana. I don't know if you've realized this yet, but if you'd been home, it's pretty likely you'd also have been killed. Before I leave here, I am going to ask Sheriff Avery to post a deputy to your home, until we can be positive you're safe. I hope you won't object."

"No, in fact I would appreciate that," Connors said.

A search of the greenhouse proved just as fruitless as those of the chicken coops. Apparently, the only building Lillian Gates's killer had entered was the shed where her body was found. When Jim returned to the house, he found the sheriff waiting for him, along with two of his deputies.

"You have any luck, Jim?" Avery asked.

"Only if you count bad luck. Or if you want to count findin' a whole heap of marijuana growin' in the greenhouse back yonder. I've already advised Ms. Connors I'm leavin' that for you to handle, as you see fit. Except for the strand of hair, some fingerprints, and a couple of things that may or may not have been handled by the perpetrator, I haven't found a single lead. How about you?"

"We haven't found a damn thing, either. There's still a couple of my deputies out there, but I'm not hoping for much."

"You never know what might turn up. Listen, Fred, I want to finish processing the little bit of evidence I have found. I'd appreciate it if you and a couple of your people could search the house while I do that."

"Of course. I forgot to mention my deputy who went for the search warrant called in. He's got it and is on his way back."

"Good. Ms. Connors, do we still have your

permission to continue searching your property until the warrant arrives?"

"Certainly, Ranger."

"Thank you again. I'll need you to remain here in the house until I return. Unfortunately, you won't be allowed to move any personal property until we've finished our search."

"I understand, Ranger."

"Fred, I know I don't have to remind you of this, but make certain you cover the entire house. Particularly look for a suicide note, or any other indication Ms. Gates might have taken her own life."

"You still believe that's a possibility, Jim?"

"Not really, but we can't afford any mistakes here. If you do come across anything, send someone for me right away."

"Will do."

Jim spent the next hour combing through the shed for further evidence. He bagged two scraps of cloth, and a piece of plastic for testing. After that, he took those items, along with the chicken, to his truck. He placed the chicken in the cooler, filled with ice, he always kept in the truck to preserve evidence. He'd take the dead bird, along with the strand of hair he'd found, to the Department of Public Safety forensics lab in Austin for DNA testing. When he returned to the house, Sheriff Avery was waiting for him.

"I'm done here, Fred," Jim said. "Gonna head for Austin to drop off the chicken and a couple other items at the lab. You didn't happen to find anythin' else here in the house, did you?"

"Not in the house, but two of my men did find these running loose," Avery answered. He handed Jim a shoebox, which had holes punched in its sides and top. "Go ahead, open it."

Jim lifted the top, discovering the box contained two-week-old chicks.

"They must have gotten loose somehow," Avery said. "Ms. Connors said their mother wouldn't take 'em back now, and the other chickens would probably peck 'em to death. We thought you should have them, so we bought 'em for you. They're yours."

"Chicks? Why in the world would I need more damn chicks? My wife and mother have plenty already. That sure wasn't my idea."

"Ah, but these two are *special,*" Avery answered. He began to laugh. "They're Speckled Ranger chicks. You have to take 'em home. The poor things have no mama. We paid for 'em, so it's not like you're takin' a bribe."

"As if you could bribe me with two chickens," Jim said. He started to say more when Avery's phone rang.

"Hold on a minute," Avery said, as he answered. "Sheriff Avery."

He listened a moment.

"Yeah? Where?"

Another pause.

"Okay, I'm still on scene at the first location. Ranger Blawcyzk is with me. We'll be there in less than fifteen minutes."

Avery clicked off the phone.

"What've you got?" Jim asked.

"Another damn dead body, that's what. Over to Pontotoc. You're not gonna believe this, but apparently, there's another dead chicken with it."

"Not funny, Fred."

"Do I look like I'm jokin'? You comin'?"

"No, you sure don't. I've just about wrapped things up here. Ms. Connors, we've got to leave you," Jim said. "There'll be a deputy here until Sheriff Avery returns, then he'll arrange for one to guard you until I feel it's no longer necessary. If you think of anything else, you've got my card. Call me or the Llano County Sheriff's office if you need anything. Fred, let's go."

Jim didn't even realize he still had the shoe box containing the chicks in his hand, until he got behind the steering wheel. He placed the box on the passenger side floor, tossed a windbreaker around it to keep it from sliding around, then followed the sheriff onto the highway.

4

A stiff northwest wind started kicking up as Jim, following the sheriff, drove to Pontotoc. Before they were halfway to their destination, it was blowing steadily at over forty miles per hour, with gusts up to sixty and higher. Blinding, wind-driven dust brought the visibility down to almost zero. Between trying to keep the sheriff's vehicle in sight, straining to see, and fighting the wind to keep his truck on the road, Jim had to slow to a crawl. Finally, the strobe lights of a parked patrol car pierced the gloom. The hulking shadows of the virtual ghost town of Pontotoc's ruins added to the ominous atmosphere.

Jim kept behind Avery as the sheriff turned onto the gravel and dirt, rutted College Street, then pulled to a stop, in front of another Llano deputy's Explorer. Behind the Explorer was a new, highly polished, black Rolls Royce Ghost sedan, which bore European license plates. Jim stopped behind it.

"No use in even tryin' to keep my hat on in this," he muttered, removing his white Stetson and tossing it on the passenger seat. He pulled a bandana from the Tahoe's center console and tied that over his nose and mouth. It wouldn't keep out all the dust, but it would help. It took all of Jim's strength to force his door open. He and Avery leaned hard against the wind as they walked up to the waiting deputy.

"Howdy, Jody," Avery said. "This here's Ranger James Blawcyzk. He's covering for Ranger Martinez. Ranger, Senior Deputy Jody Kennedy. What've you got, Jody?"

"The body of a male in that abandoned truck over there," Kennedy answered, pointing at the vehicle. "I didn't open that thing. Figured you'd want to take a look before I did, Ranger. There's another abandoned truck a ways beyond that one, which you can't hardly see for all this damned dust. I thought there might be another body in the second vehicle, so I went to check it. That's where I found a dead chicken. I know the place y'all were at's a chicken farm, so I thought there might be a connection. I get my eggs from that farm. Darned shame one of those women is dead. They're both nice ladies."

"Those people in the Rolls find the body?" Jim asked.

"Yeah, they did. You want to talk with 'em right now?"

"I would, but with this storm blowin' up, I'd better take a quick look at the body first, then have you try'n cover it with a tarp, if you can find a way to keep one down in this wind."

"Most of the windows are still in that junker, so I'll get 'er done somehow."

"*Gracias*, Deputy. I appreciate that," Jim said. "C'mon, Fred, let's go take a look."

Jim and the sheriff walked over to the first vehicle Kennedy had indicated, a late 1960s model International Travelall, one of the predecessors to modern SUVs. The truck's turquoise and white paint was faded, its hood and most of the engine parts were long gone, but, as the deputy had said, except for the front vent windows, and the front passenger door window, the glass was still intact. Even through the bandana, Jim could smell the stench of decaying flesh coming from inside.

A quick glance into the Travelall confirmed what his nose had already told him. The body it contained, lying across the rusted springs of the rotted-out front seat, was badly decomposed. Its head was twisted at an awkward angle, indicating a probable broken neck. Jim wondered, for a moment, whether Deputy Kennedy had waited to give him the chance to examine the body first, as he'd said, or just didn't want to deal with the sight and smell of a corpse in an advanced state of decomposition. Jim took several quick pictures of the corpse, before the wind became too strong to continue.

"There's not a helluva lot we can do here, Fred," Jim shouted, in order to be heard above the howling winds. "This one's gotta go to the coroner. Order up a hook, and we'll have it take this wreck over to the coroner's office with the body still inside. The coroner can meet us there. I'll take a preliminary look inside the truck once the wind dies down, then finish goin' through it back in Llano. Same for the other truck."

"All right, Jim. Damn, this wind's really gettin' worse. I'm hearin' some thunder off in the distance, too. I think we're about to be hit real hard, with one helluva storm."

"Doesn't really matter as far as collectin' evidence goes. Anything that might've been out here, footprints or tire tracks, somethin' that might've been left behind, has long since been obliterated. We'll get back to the folks who found the body. Unless this storm blows itself out real quick, we could be stuck here for a while. It's impossible to even think about drivin' right now. When you call for the hooks, might as well tell 'em not to leave Llano until the weather clears some. Get in my truck, and we'll talk things over while we wait for this storm to blow over. You can tell your deputy to hold off tryin' to cover the body until the storm's gone past."

"You've got it, Jim."

The first large drops of rain were spattering the dust when Jim got back to his truck, and the luxury sedan. He tapped on what he thought was the driver's window of the Rolls Royce. It was lowered halfway, to reveal a man wearing a chauffeur's uniform sitting on the opposite side, behind the right-hand drive sedan's steering wheel.

"Texas Ranger Jim Blawcyzk," Jim said, hurriedly. "I understand you folks are the ones who found the body. I'll need to ask you some questions; however, I'm afraid you'll have to wait this storm out right here, along with me. It's far too dangerous to drive. I'll be in my truck until the rain and wind subside."

"Right, Guv'nor," the chauffeur answered, in a heavy Liverpudlian accent. "Allow me a moment while I inform the Earl."

He pressed a button on the steering wheel, then spoke into a microphone mounted in the dashboard.

"M'Lord?"

"Yes, Stephan?"

"There's a gentleman outside the automobile who appears to be a member of the state constabulary. He's advising that travel will be too hazardous to attempt, until the weather clears somewhat."

"That will be fine, Stephan. We are quite comfortable right here, at least for the moment. Unless, of course, one of those dreadful tornadoes I've heard of descends upon us."

"Tell your employer the odds of that are very

small. We'd be far more likely to get into an accident if we attempted to drive to shelter," Jim said.

A plexiglass panel between the chauffeur and rear passenger compartment descended silently.

"I heard you, good sir," a voice from the back, with a clipped British accent, said. "Remaining in place is quite acceptable. And this storm is exhilarating, to say the least. We seldom have rough weather like this back home in the United Kingdom. Mostly, we have dreary fog and drizzle, for weeks on end."

"If you say so, sir," Jim answered. "I'm gettin' back in my truck before it hits full force, and I drown standin' up. You folks just stay hunkered down until I'm back."

Before Jim could duck into the shelter of his Tahoe, a bolt of lightning struck, far too close for comfort, immediately followed by a tremendous clap of thunder. He jumped into the truck and slammed his door shut just as the heavens opened up in a torrential cloudburst. The sharp odors of ozone and brimstone hung in the air.

"Damn, Jim, I thought that one might've gotten you," Avery said. "You all right?"

"I'll let you know, as soon as my ears stop ringin'," Jim answered. "Sure hope you didn't sit on my hat."

"Nah, it's in the back seat, along with the chicks."

"The chicks! I plumb forgot about those."

Jim reached into the back seat and grabbed the shoebox. He removed the cover and breathed a sigh of relief to see the two chicks were huddled in a corner of the box, frightened, but alive. One of them looked at him and gave a tentative peep.

"Poor little fellers. I'll bet you're scared to death," Jim said. "Probably hungry and thirsty, too. Lemme see what I can do about that."

He took a half-empty bottle of water from the center console, opened it, and poured the cap almost full. He offered it to the chicks, who hesitated, then took several swallows.

"There ya go. Now, let's see if I can come up with somethin' for you to munch on. Don't have any feed for you. Lemme think a minute. Ah, I know."

Jim opened the ever-present can of cashews he kept within easy reach. This can was almost empty, so it was easy for him to dig to the bottom and come up with some crumbs. He scattered those on the bottom of the box. The chicks eagerly pecked at them.

"That'll hold you until I can get some proper feed for you," Jim said. "At least you'll have somethin' in your bellies."

"Gee, I'm sure glad to see you didn't want those critters," Avery said, with a laugh.

"I didn't, but I'm not gonna let 'em starve to

death. Besides, my wife and mother'll dote on these things."

Another bolt of lightning struck nearby, flowed by a clap of thunder and gust of wind that rocked Jim's truck.

"This is almost as bad as the storm they had here back in 2016, that knocked down what was left standin' of the old San Fernando Academy," Avery said.

"I knew there was somethin' missin' from the last time I passed through here," Jim said. "The school's walls are gone. There's nothin' left of 'em."

"Nope, not any longer. They're nothin' but a pile of rubble now. 'Course, the only folks who really noticed were those who live right around here, and maybe a few tourists who enjoy visitin' ghost towns. I'm amazed the Post Office wasn't shut down years ago. The only new sign of life is a winery that opened up a few years back. That, the little store, and a few loners and ranchers. The whole town should have dried up and blown away, a long time ago. It never came back after the fire in '47 that burned most of the downtown, such as it was."

"You've gotta admit though, it's a damn fine place to hide a body," Jim said. "With this storm, I could swear some of those ruins are haunted. I can see ghosts in the windows with every lightning flash. Y'know, I'm really interested to

58

hear what those rich English folks are doin' out here in the middle of nowhere, and how they stumbled upon the corpse. It's definitely been here for quite some time."

"Yeah, that is a bit curious."

"Fred, this whole day has been more'n a bit curious. Since I haven't had a chance to examine this scene yet, I can't say for certain, but if there's a dead chicken in that other truck, like your deputy says, odds are whoever committed these murders are one and the same person."

"That still leaves a whole lotta questions, Jim."

"Tell me about it. Who, and why, for starters. What was the connection, if any, between the victims? Is it someone local? How much do you know about Mary Connors, and Lillian Gates?"

"Not a whole lot. They were pretty quiet, mostly ran their farm and kept to themselves. When they did come into town, they were friendly enough, I guess. I can tell you we never had to go out to their place for any complaints. Why? Do you think Connors killed Gates?"

Jim shook his head.

"I can't discount the possibility, not at this point, but I don't think so. I found no evidence indicating she did, but I did find a couple things that tell me someone else was in that shed. One, I found a strand of long, brown hair. Both Gates and Connors kept their hair cropped short. Gates's was auburn, Connors's dyed blonde.

Neither one's a match for the hair I found. I also picked up a couple of partial fingerprints. Once we get the women's prints, I'm almost positive they won't be a match."

"Those things you found could belong to anyone, not the killer," Avery pointed out. "They're hardly proof, certainly not good enough to convince a prosecutor to press charges and bring an indictment."

"Not on their own, but once they're tested for DNA, and if I can find whoever they belong to, a match would pretty much establish a connection. Particularly if the lab can get some samples off the rope used to hang Gates. Meantime, since this storm doesn't seem to be lettin' up, I'm gonna take a nap. It's been a long day already, and it sure ain't gonna get any shorter."

"You can sleep through *this?*" Avery asked, as another bolt of lightning struck too close for comfort, and thunder boomed yet again.

"I can sleep through just about anything," Jim answered. He reclined his seat, stretched out his legs, and pulled his hat over his eyes. Sure enough, despite the wind buffeting the Tahoe, the vivid lightning and crashing thunder, within two minutes he was sound asleep. He awakened when the storm moved on, the thunder now rumbling far in the distance to the southeast, the rain little more than a hard drizzle.

"Reckon we can get back to work," he said,

then yawned and stretched. "I'd better call my wife, and let her know I won't be comin' home tonight."

"I still can't believe you were able to sleep through all that," Avery said. "A few times, I thought for certain the damn wind was gonna blow this truck right over."

Jim gave Avery a backhanded slap to his stomach.

"No worries there, Fred. Not with that gut you're growin'. We were weighted down good and proper. Time to cut back on the ribs and brisket there, partner."

Jim laughed, then hit Kim's number on his phone. Kim's rang twice, then she answered.

"Hi, Jim. Where are you at?" she said.

"Hi, honey. I'm way out in a ghost town called Pontotoc. Just finished waitin' out a wicked thunderstorm. I'm afraid I won't be home tonight. It turns out I've got two possible homicides to deal with, which may be connected. I'm just about to start investigating the one here. Once I'm done questioning a few folks, and combing through the scene, I've got to head back to Llano to process a couple of vehicles, which I'm havin' towed there, for evidence. I'll get a room for the night in town, and grab a couple hours' sleep. After that, tomorrow I'll be with the coroner while he performs autopsies on the victims, then I'll have some more people to question. Once I'm finished doin' that, I'll need to drive to Austin, to drop off some possible evidence at the lab for testing. I'm sorry, honey. I didn't want you to keep supper for me, or to worry."

"I've gotten used to your crazy hours, Jim," Kim answered. "Just stay safe."

"I will," Jim promised her. "How did your day go?"

"Apparently much better than yours. The new clients I mentioned signed a two-year consulting contract with me. Your mother and I took them to lunch at El Morocco to celebrate. I hope you've eaten."

"Haven't had the chance yet. Don't worry. I'll grab a bite soon as I get back to Llano. I've got plenty of cashews and Dr Pepper to hold me over until then. Listen, Kim, I've gotta run. Tell Ma goodnight, and kiss Josh for me."

"All right, honey. I love you."

"Love you, too. I'll see you sometime tomorrow." He clicked the disconnect button.

"Okay, Fred," Jim said, turning to Avery, "I'll go talk with our British friends. While I'm doin' that, I'd appreciate you talking to however many people do live in this place, to see if any of 'em noticed something wrong, like a stranger passin' through, or a vehicle that didn't belong to any of the locals. Tell your deputy to forget about covering the body. Have him tape off this whole area, maybe call in a couple more units to keep curious folks away."

"You mean all eight or ten of 'em?" Avery asked. "Hell, hardly anybody even drives by here, let alone lives here."

He laughed.

"Yeah, I can see your point," Jim said. "Still, until I have my work done, let's be sure any- one who does happen by is kept away from tramplin' over the scene. I'll give everything a quick look-see before the hooks arrive, and dust both vehicles for prints. After that, I'll want both those trucks covered completely with tarps, and kept covered until we're back in Llano. Send your deputy to me soon as you get done with him. We'll escort the hooks back. Let's get started."

"Sure, Jim. It won't take me all that long to round up the residents. Most of 'em'll probably come out to see what's up, now that the storm's over. If anyone has information that might be helpful, I'll bring them over to you."

"That'll work."

They got out of the Tahoe. Jim tapped on the driver's window again, this time the correct, right-hand-side one.

"Yes, Guv'nor?" the chauffeur said.

"I'm ready to interview y'all shortly, as soon as I examine the body," Jim said. "I'll identify myself once more. Texas Ranger James

Blawcyzk, Company F. Might I ask your names?"

Before the chauffeur could answer, one of the back windows was lowered. A man in his early fifties, who had light green eyes, silver-gray hair, and a precisely trimmed moustache, stuck his head out the window.

"It would be preferable to address me directly, sir," he said. "My name is Reginald Pierpont Hannaford-Smythe, Earl of Wessington. My wife, Countess Olivia Jane Hannaford-Smythe, is accompanying me."

"Thank you, sir."

"The Earl is properly addressed as 'Your Lord', and the Countess 'Your Lady', officer," the chauffeur said, the tone of his voice making it plain he felt he was talking to an inferior.

"Well, y'see, we're not quite so formal down here in Texas," Jim answered, purposely adding depth to his Texas twang. "We don't cotton much to folks throwin' around high-falutin' titles. That's why we had a revolution, way back in 1776, to break away from such nonsense. 'Course, that's all in the past now, and our countries are friends, and pardners. So if y'all don't mind, I'll just call you Mr. or Mrs. Hannaford-Smythe. My last name is pronounced BLUH-zhick. I know it's a bit hard to wrap your tongue around."

"Of course. That will be fine, Ranger," Hannaford-Smythe answered. To the chauffeur, he continued, "Stephan, I do wish you'd stop being so tiresome. I've reminded you several times already that in this country, peerage, and titles of nobility or royalty, are not recognized. If someone wants to address us as Lord and Lady, that is fine. If they prefer not to, that is also perfectly acccptablc. Do you understand?

"Yes, m'Lord."

"Good."

"Ranger, both my wife and I are prepared to answer your questions," Hannaford-Smythe said.

"I appreciate that, sir," Jim answered. "However, I do have to perform an examination of the deceased, along with a search of the vehicle where the body was found, before I can allow them to be taken to the county seat for further processing. I apologize I must detain you for a short time longer, but I've got to do that before I talk with y'all. I promise I will be back with you as quickly as possible."

"That's perfectly all right," Hannaford-Smythe answered. "The Countess and I are in no hurry to reach a destination. In fact, with your permission, we would like to observe as you go about your duties."

Jim took off his Stetson and ran a hand through his hair, then rubbed his jaw before answering.

"I reckon that will be all right, as long as you stay on the road. I can't allow you to touch anything, or perhaps disturb any evidence. Also, the few folks who live around here are gonna be mighty curious about you. If any of them bother you, just let me know."

"I doubt they will. And it will be a chance for use to meet some genuine Texans," Hannaford-Smythe answered. "I assure you, my wife and I will stay out of your hair . . . of which I am quite jealous, I might add." He laughed, and lifted his driving cap to reveal a receding hairline, the rest of his scalp barely covered with thin, gray hair, which was in stark contrast to the unruly thatch of thick, blonde hair covering Jim's head.

"Yeah, but if this was the old days, and we were attacked by a band of Comanches, I'd be the one to lose his hair, not you," Jim said, also laughing. "Well, I'd better get to work. If you'd like to watch, c'mon."

"Just lead the way."

Carrying his evidence kit, along with his BDU, Jim walked over to the Travelall. He told the Hannaford-Smythes to remain several feet from the vehicle, then donned the BDU, nitrile gloves, and booties. He also covered his mouth and nose with an anti-microbial mask. He turned on his recorder, dictated the usual basic information, took photos of the Travelall, and the ground around it, from all angles, then opened the passenger door. Dust and dirt, blown into the International by the fierce winds, now covered the body.

"I am now performing a perfunctory examination of the corpse," he said into his recorder. "Body is badly decomposed, so much so any determination of the cause of death, age, and other specifics will need to be determined by autopsy.

"In addition, the storm which just struck the area has contaminated any possible evidence with sand and water blown into the vehicle. Any physical evidence outside the vehicle where the body was found has also been badly degraded, if not completely obliterated.

"However, preliminary observation indicates the deceased suffered a broken neck, most likely not inside the vehicle where the body was discovered. The body possibly could be that of a Hispanic male; however, the skin is too badly discolored and deteriorated. Due to its condition, there is no possible way to even estimate a time of death, although that certainly occurred no more three or four days ago, probably less, perhaps as shortly as yesterday. Decomposition inside a vehicle, in this extreme heat, would be rapid.

"From the position of the body, lying across the front seat of the vehicle, it would seem victim was placed inside sometime after death occurred. I am having the vehicle towed, with the body remaining inside, to the Llano County impound for further examination, at which point, the deceased will be transported to the Llano County

Coroner's Office for forensic testing and autopsy.

"There is a second abandoned vehicle which contains a dead chicken, which is a possible tie-in to the previous apparent homicide I am currently investigating. That vehicle will also be towed to the Llano County impound."

He turned off his recorder when he saw Sheriff Avery approaching.

"Jim, I've got two rotation flatbeds comin' up from Pepe and Pedro's Auto Body in Llano. They should be here within twenty minutes. You find anything?"

"Nope. The body's too far gone to do much with it, until the autopsy. The damn storm either contaminated or blew away any possible evidence. Once Pepe's gets here, I'll have 'em tarp the trucks, then once they get 'em back to Llano, I'll turn the body over to the coroner, and go through the vehicles there. I'm just gonna dust this truck for prints, take a quick look in the pickup, then talk with the Hannaford-Smythes."

"Anything I can do in the meantime?"

"Just keep on pluggin' away. Basically, the same thing we're doin' down at the other scene. Make certain your deputies talk to everyone who lives around here, then get the names, addresses, and phone numbers of those folks, and your people's notes, to me for follow-up. In a place this small, someone should have seen somethin'. I'll also want another roadblock put in place, this one for forty-eight hours. Stop everyone who comes by. You know the routine."

"Unfortunately, I sure do. I'll have my deputies look around for anything out of place, too."

"That's good. Meet me back at my truck. We'll talk with the Earl and his wife there. I'll explain to them what's going on."

"Will do."

Avery walked off, to pass along Jim's instructions to his deputies.

Jim went over to the Hannaford-Smythes.

"I apologize, but I have to ask you folks to remain here a bit longer," he told them. "The tow trucks are on their way, and will be here shortly. I'm gonna take a quick look in the old pickup over yonder, then I'll be able to ask you my questions. You're both more than welcome to wait either in your vehicle, or mine, rather than out here in the blazin' sun. If you're not careful, you could get a nasty burn."

"We'll be just fine, Ranger, but thank you for your concern," Hannaford-Smythe answered. "I have my cap, and the Countess has her bonnet and brolly. Those will protect us from the sun. Besides, watching you work is rather fascinating. Unless you object, we'll remain right here."

"That's fine; however, if you're going to remain in Texas for any length of time, you might want to consider purchasing a cowboy hat. That cap you're wearing won't protect your ears, or the back of your neck, hardly at all," Jim answered. "I won't be very long. Whatever happened took place some time ago, so the forensic work which needs to be performed will have to be done at the Department of Public Service lab in Austin. Between the amount of time that elapsed, plus exposure of the site to the elements, there's not much left for me to work with."

"Understood."

Jim walked over to the abandoned pickup, a badly faded white International of about the same vintage as the Travelall. The bed was full of debris, including a flat spare tire. Unlike the Travelall, none of the pickup's windows still had their glass. Jim looked through the passenger door window frame, then opened the door, its hinges squealing in protest. The door refused to budge, until he gave it a hard yank, forcing it halfway open. On the seat were the skeletal remains of a large, white-feathered chicken. Jim took photos of that, then sealed it in a large, plastic bag, to be examined later. He then took more photos of the truck, both inside and out, dusted it for prints, then sifted through the sand piled inside and surrounding it, hoping to find some piece of evidence the apparent killer had left behind. By the time he finished, the tow trucks were pulling up. Jim gestured to the drivers to join him when they got out of their vehicles.

"Afternoon, men," he said. "I'm Ranger James

Blawcyzk. I appreciate your getting here as fast as possible."

"No problem, Ranger," one of the drivers answered. "I'm Pepe, and this here's my brother Pedro. What d'ya need us to do?"

"I need those two heaps behind me hauled back to the county impound yard. You'll have to swing by the county coroner's office en route with the Travelall, 'cause there's a body inside that needs to be removed. Me'n the sheriff will escort you boys back to town. I have to warn you, you'll need strong stomachs, because the corpse has been inside that truck long enough it's pretty far gone. I'll give you a couple of masks to help block out the stench, and protective gloves, before you start to work. Lemme know if either of you thinks you can't handle it."

"Ranger, we've been in this business for over twenty years," Pedro answered. "There ain't much we haven't seen. We'll do just fine. Just tell us how you want this handled."

"I want those vehicles wrapped up in tarps, real tight. Don't touch anything inside 'em that you don't have to. Soon as you've got them loaded, we'll start for town. While you're working, I've got a couple of witnesses to interview. See the sheriff or his deputy if you need any assistance."

"Sure, Ranger," Pepe answered. "C'mon, Pedro, let's get started."

"Hold on just a second," Jim said. "Don't forget these."

He pulled two masks, along with two pairs of gloves, from one of his pockets and handed them to the tow truck operators.

"Right. *Gracias*. We're obliged," Pedro said, as he took the protective items.

While the tow truck operators went to work, Jim put the chicken's remains in the cooler in his truck, then rejoined the Hannaford-Smythes. Sheriff Avery was already with them.

"Thank you for your patience," Jim said. "It won't be long until you can be on your way. I will require a way to reach you later, if need be. Where are you staying?"

"Actually, we haven't chosen a spot for tonight," Hannaford-Smythe answered. "Also, as long as we are in your country, please, call me Reginald, and my wife Olivia."

"Won't that just unravel Stephan's twine?" Mrs. Hannaford-Smythe said, with a slight smile.

"That's of no concern," her husband answered. "Stephan had bloody well get used to the fact we are no longer in the United Kingdom, and won't return home for many months, at the very least." To Jim and Avery, he continued, "You see, Olivia and I are on an extended tour of your marvelous country, particularly here in the West. We plan on traveling throughout the United States, then Canada, for at least two years, perhaps longer, which is why we had our own automobile shipped over. One thing we are really appreciating is the price of petrol. It's far less expensive than it is on our side of the pond. If it's not asking too much, might we trouble you gentlemen for a suggestion where to stay tonight?"

"It's no trouble; however, the nearest hotels are down in Llano," Avery answered. "There's a Best Western, a Days Inn, two other private-owned places that I wouldn't even use to lock up a prisoner they're so bad, and a few bed and breakfasts."

"We don't want a chain's facility, or some cookie-cutter type of place," Hannaford-Smythe answered. "We are trying to get a real feel for your state. Something where we could get an in-depth chance to understand the history of this area would be preferable."

Jim and Avery looked at each other.

"The Dabbs!" they said, in unison.

"The Dabbs?" Hannaford-Smythe said.

"The Dabbs Railroad Hotel. It's the last surviving Texas Railroad and River Hotel," Jim said. "It's now a bed and breakfast. However, it might be a bit too rustic for your taste."

"How so?" Mrs. Hannaford-Smythe asked.

"Well, ma'am, it's been modernized to current safety standards, with an up-to-date kitchen, but it's still very much set up as it was originally built, back in 1907," Avery answered. "Most of the bedroom furnishings are original, or from the period when passenger trains still traversed almost the entire state, connecting small towns, farming and ranching communities. The Dabbs was the last stop on the rail line connecting Llano to Austin. If you wanted to continue west from Llano, you had to go on horseback, or take a stagecoach. Automobiles were still few and far between back then. Most roads through the Hill Country weren't suitable for motorized travel, anyway. They were little more than trails. The hotel's accommodations are preserved almost exactly as they were back in the late nineteenth and early twentieth centuries. That means no air conditioning, breakfast is served in a common dining room, and no television. Most importantly, there's no private bathroom for each bedroom. There's one bath for every two or three rooms to share, usually across the hall. The Dabbs is clean and comfortable, but hardly luxurious."

"The sheriff's right," Jim said. "My wife and I spent a weekend there a couple of years back. It's a fun place to stay, but not exactly the Waldorf-Astoria in New York City. In addition, supposedly the place is haunted. Some folks claim you can even hear the piano on the front porch being played in the middle of the night, but no one's at the keyboard. On the other hand, the back porch has a lovely view of the river, and is a wonderful place to unwind and enjoy the cool evening breeze. It's quite relaxing. Oh, and if you're really into Texas history, it was a hangout for lawmen, miners, and outlaws of all sorts, including bank and train robbers. The most famous of those are undoubtedly Bonnie and Clyde. The Dabbs was a favorite haunt of theirs."

"You mean Bonnie Parker, the infamous robber and murderess, and her paramour, Clyde Barrow?" Mrs. Hannaford-Smythe said.

"Yes, ma'am, those would be the ones," Jim answered. "The hotel even has a picture of them taken in front of the place."

"That's marvelous. I've always been fascinated by her. Reginald, we *must* spend some time at the establishment, don't you agree?"

"Of course, Olivia. It sounds absolutely splendid. Since the place is supposedly haunted, that makes it even more intriguing. Sheriff, are there other interesting things and places to explore in this region?" Hannaford-Smythe asked.

"There are plenty of 'em. We're right smack dab in the middle of the Texas Hill Country. There's lots of historic sites, as well as outdoor activities, shopping, the Texas Wine Trail, or merely relaxing and enjoying the scenery. One spot you shouldn't miss is Enchanted Rock. You can climb to the top of it, and see for miles in every direction."

"Then it's settled. We'll make the, um . . ."

"Dabbs," Jim offered.

"The Dabbs our headquarters while we're exploring this area," Hannaford-Smythe concluded.

"That also means I'll know where to reach you if I need to get in touch later," Jim said. He glanced up at the sun, which was well past halfway on its descent to the western horizon.

"Listen, it's getting late," he said. "The wrecker drivers are just about done loading up, too. Since I'll be spending the night in Llano anyway, I'll also get a room at the Dabbs. That way, I'll only need to get some basic information from you folks here, then I can finish interviewing you back at the hotel, where we'll all be more comfortable. Is that agreeable?"

"That will be fine," Hannaford-Smythe answered.

"Good. I am going to request that you stay with us on the trip to Llano. Fred, could you have one of your deputies come along with us, and lead the Hannaford-Smythes to their hotel once we reach town?"

"Sure, Jim. I'll have Jody do that."

"*Gracias.* I'll only be a few more minutes. Just have to ask our friends here a couple of questions, then once the vehicles are loaded, I want to search the ground under where they were parked. While I do that, see if there's anyone your people feel I should talk with. After that, we'll be on our way."

"You got it."

Jim turned his attention back to the Hannaford-Smythes.

"I'm ready. First, do I have permission to record your statements, including one from your chauffeur?"

"Yes," Hannaford-Smythe answered.

"Thank you."

Jim turned his recorder on.

"Continuing my investigation into an apparent homicide on College Street in Pontotoc, Llano County, approximately at the site of the former San Fernando Academy. This is a brief interview with the persons who found the body, which will be continued later today, after our return to Llano. First, may I have your names and home address?"

"Of course, Ranger. Reginald Hannaford-Smythe, Earl of Wessington, in the United Kingdom. My address is Bethpage Manor in that township."

"I am Olivia Hannaford-Smythe, Countess of Wessington. Reginald is my husband."

"And you, sir?" Jim said, looking directly at the chauffeur.

"My name is Stephan George Anthony Putnam, the Earl and Countess's driver and automobile caretaker. M'Lord and Lady own a fleet of several vehicles, in addition to this one."

"I see. Thank you. Mr. Hannaford-Smythe, it is my understanding you and your wife are on an extended tour of the United States. Is that correct?"

"Yes."

"The reason you stopped here in Pontotoc?"

"We were exploring the back roads in this region. When we stumbled upon this town, we discovered the ruins of its former center. Since we're interested in old abandoned towns and ruins, such as the many we have of ancient castles and manor houses in the United Kingdom, and are particularly interested in Western United States ghost towns, we knew we had to stop."

"And when you did, you discovered the body of the deceased."

"That is correct, sir. Actually, my wife found it first."

"I see. Mrs. Hannaford-Smythe, would you relate for me exactly how you found the body?"

"Certainly. While my husband was rummaging through the rubble of a tumbled-down stone structure, I decided to look inside the abandoned vehicles parked nearby, hoping I might find something of interest. I never expected to discover a dead body. It was quite shocking."

"I'm certain it was," Jim answered. "What did you do after you made the discovery?"

"I called my husband over to join me. Then, we summoned the authorities. Fortunately, we were able to obtain cell phone service, even way out here in the wilderness. That meant we didn't have to disturb anyone to use their phone."

"Did either one of you touch the vehicle containing the body, inside or out, or any of its contents?"

"No, neither of us. We simply returned to our vehicle to await the arrival of the police."

"Did your chauffeur observe your discovery?"

"No, Ranger, he remained in our automobile the entire time.'" Hannaford-Smythe answered. "I'm afraid Stephan isn't the adventurous type."

"I know this question may seem a bit unnecessary, since the body you found has been in this location for more than a day, but did either of you see anything, or anyone, you believe might have some connection to the deceased?"

"No, neither of us. Once my wife showed me her gruesome discovery, we immediately returned to our vehicle, summoned the police, and waited for their arrival."

"I thank the both of you for your cooperation," Jim said. "I will continue this questioning in Llano."

He switched off his recorder.

"I'll work as quickly as I can," he said. "I'm obliged for your patience. Once we get rollin', it'll take about a half-hour to reach Llano. That's a bit longer than normal, but we won't be able to travel as fast as usual, due to having the wreckers with us. I'm gonna send Deputy Kennedy to remain with you until we leave."

"That's understandable. It is we who are

grateful to you, Ranger, for your courtesy to us," Mrs. Hannaford-Smythe said.

Jim returned to where the two old Internationals had been abandoned. Both were now loaded on flatbeds, wrapped in blue tarps, and strapped down tightly. Pepe and Pedro were standing alongside their trucks.

"We're all set, whenever you are, Ranger," Pepe said.

"I see that. You have any trouble loadin' those heaps up?"

"Not at all," Pedro answered. "It's not like we had to worry about doin' any damage to 'em. All we had to do was drag 'em on the beds, cover 'em up, and strap 'em down."

"The one with the body was a tad rank, though," Pepe added.

"Ya think?" Jim said. "I hate to keep you waitin', but now that those vehicles are out of the way, I've got to check the ground that was underneath 'em, just on the slim chance I might find somethin' useful. Soon as I've done that, unless the sheriff has found any witnesses I need to talk with, we'll hit the road. I'll take the lead, with the black Rolls behind me. Deputy Kennedy will be behind the Rolls, then you two follow him. Sheriff Avery will bring up the rear. We'll be usin' our emergency lights, and sirens when we need 'em. We won't be stoppin' for any traffic lights."

80

"Hell, the whole damn town's only got two lights, and we'll only be goin' by one of those," Pepe said, laughing. "You mind if we have a cold *cerveza* while we're waitin', Ranger?"

"Long as it's no more'n one, it'll be okay."

"*Gracias*. A man builds up a right powerful thirst in this heat."

"I promise, I won't keep you waitin' all that long."

"Take your time. The county's payin' us by the hour," Pepe said, with a grin.

"Only if I approve the charges, since they'll be billin' the state," Jim shot back, grinning.

Jim headed over to the spots where the Internationals had been left to rust away, for who knew how many years. The ground they'd sheltered was compacted, and hard as concrete, covered only with a thin layer of loose sand. A small, shiny object glinted from near where the Travelall's right front tire had rested. Jim took a pair of tweezers from his pocket, used those to pick up the object, then studied it carefully, from all angles.

"Huh," he grunted, as he slid the object into a baggie, then sealed it. "If that dead *hombre* is Mexican, as my gut tells me he is, this would sure tie in with that."

Lastly, Jim looked through a rusted piece of farm machinery, that had been left to rot, but came up empty-handed. When further searching turned up nothing more of interest, Jim headed back to his Tahoe, and stripped off his BDU.

"You find anythin', Jim?" Avery asked.

"Maybe. I'll show it to you when we get back to town, and see what you think. Anybody your people talked to see anythin' at all?"

Avery shook his head.

"Nope. Not a damn one of 'em claims to have seen anyone near those trucks, or the old school, for weeks. No strangers have gone into the store, or the Post Office, either. I'm afraid we're at a dead end, there."

"Well, just have your deputies get their transcripts to me, so I can follow up if I need to. And if anyone who gets stopped at the roadblock recollects anything, I'll want to know right away. We've done everything we can here. Let's get goin'."

Jim had left his truck running, both for his own comfort, and to keep the chicks from literally roasting to death. They were peeping when he opened the door and settled into the driver's seat. Jim took the top off the shoebox and tossed them more cashew crumbs.

"I'm sorry, fellers. I'll get you some decent feed soon as I can, I promise. Once I get you home, Kim and my ma'll make all this up to you."

Jim popped open a can of Dr Pepper, put the Tahoe in gear, and drove slowly off. The few residents of Pontotoc watched with morbid curiosity as the strange procession of police vehicles, a Rolls Royce, and flatbed wreckers turned onto Texas 71, then rolled out of sight.

Once the caravan reached Llano, Deputy Kennedy split off, to lead the Hannaford-Smythes to their lodging. Jim, the wrecker drivers, and the sheriff continued on to the Llano County coroner's office. Coroner Maurice LaPointe heard them arrive. The overhead door to the morgue's garage was already open by the time Pepe backed up to it.

"Howdy, Fred," he said, as soon as Avery got out of his SUV. You're sure keepin' me busy this week, and it's only Monday. What've you got now?"

"I'll let the Ranger explain it to you," Avery answered.

"Maurice, this one's gonna be tough to figure out," Jim said. "I've got a badly decomposed body, which was inside an abandoned car in the sun, up in Pontotoc. I'm not even certain of the race. I'm just hopin' you can even come up with enough to identify the victim."

"Boy howdy, Ranger Blawcyzk, I hope this isn't a sign of things to come, while you're taking over for Ranger Martinez," LaPointe said.

"That makes two of us. How soon can you get started with the autopsies?"

"If it's all the same to you, first thing in the morning. I've got another one I'm in the middle of, a car wreck victim who's a mangled, bloody mess. After that, I really need to have my supper, and get some sleep."

"I'd have preferred tonight, but since I've got some more things to work on, that'll be okay," Jim answered. "I'll meet you here then."

"Appreciate that, Ranger."

Once the body was in the morgue, the two Internationals were dropped off inside the Llano County Sheriff's Department garage.

"Fred, I'm gonna let these go until later tonight," Jim said. "I want to finish talking with the Hannaford-Smythes first, then clean up and get some supper, since I know most of the restaurants in this town close before nine o'clock. You gonna call it a night?"

"I reckon I will. I've gotta agree with you. After nine, most of the sidewalks in Llano are rolled up for the night. I'll make certain my dispatcher knows you'll be back. Anything else you need right now?"

"Yeah, now that you mention it. I need to find a feed store, to pick up a bag of feed for those chicks you stuck me with. Who knows, they might turn out to be evidence. Maybe the killer picked 'em up and turned 'em loose. I realize this sounds plumb loco, but there's a slim chance he left some DNA traces behind on their down."

"There's two in town, Lyssy and Eckel, or

Llano Feeds. Lyssy and Eckel mostly sell the feeds they manufacture, while Llano carries most of the national brands."

"That'll be good enough until I get 'em home. I'm not interested in some expensive custom blend. My wife and mother'll be takin' care of those birds anyway. What times does Llano Feeds open?"

"Usually at eight, but sometimes a bit earlier."

"That's fine. I'll make a quick stop there, then head on over to the morgue. Hey, I nearly forgot. Take a look at this, and tell me what you think."

Jim removed the plastic bag holding the object he'd found alongside of where the abandoned Travelall had been parked, from his shirt pocket, and handed it to the sheriff.

"This looks like a spur for a fightin' cock," Avery said.

"That's what it is, all right. You happen to know of any cock-fightin' rings in these parts?"

Avery shrugged.

"They're out there, all right. Tryin' to find 'em and shut 'em down is about as easy as catchin' a Texas twister in a bottle. The organizers keep moving around. They'll be in one spot this week, then the next be in another place miles away. And of course, no one'll talk about 'em, for fear of gettin' beaten half to death, or worse. You think the *hombre* in Pontotoc was involved in cock-fightin'?"

"Either him, or the killer," Jim answered. "That means I'll need one of your deputies to go back up there, and question everyone in the area to see if they know of any cock-fightin' rings, and where the fights take place."

"You want me to assign Jody Kennedy as your assistant, until the killer is run down?" Avery asked. "He's my best investigator."

"I'd appreciate that, Fred."

"Consider it done. I'll let him know. You want him at the autopsies with you?"

"I sure do."

"Then he'll be there. I will, too, if it's okay."

"Of course it is. Although, I would imagine once you get back to your office, you'll find a bunch of damn reporters waitin' for you. News of the first suspicious death must have gotten out by now. Don't tell 'em any more than you have to."

"They won't get much outta me, don't worry about that. I'll see you tomorrow. *Buenas noches*, Jim."

"G'night, Fred."

Jim drove down Bessemer Avenue toward the Llano River, passed the end of the long-abandoned railroad tracks, turned left onto Train Station Drive, then right, just before the former station, onto East Burnet Street, and pulled into the Dabbs Railroad Hotel's driveway. He parked alongside the Hannaford-Smythes' Rolls-Royce, took the shoebox containing the chicks, along with the duffle bag which held his spare clothes, and went inside. The young woman behind the front desk greeted him with a warm smile.

"You must be the Texas Ranger Deputy Kennedy told me to expect," she said. "I'm Mary. Welcome to the Dabbs."

"I must be, and thank you," Jim answered. "I hope you've got a room available. Also, would you happen to have a larger box I can put these chicks in? I have to hang onto 'em, as they might be evidence in a case I'm investigating. I'd also appreciate it if you happen to have any bread crumbs to spare, until I can get them the proper feed tomorrow. Also, since I'll need to be here in town for most of the day tomorrow, I'd appreciate it if I could leave the chicks in your care until tomorrow afternoon."

"We do," Mary said. "In fact, it's a slow week. We have no weddings or other events scheduled. The only other guests are the Earl and Countess of Wessington, and their chauffeur. It's so exciting to have actual members of the English nobility staying here at our little old hotel. Their car is probably worth more than this entire property. Oh, I'm sorry for prattling on so. You wanted a room. Except for the SR and Rio Grande rooms, which the Earl and Countess have taken, you have your choice of any room in the hotel. There should be an empty box in the kitchen you can use for the chicks. I'll bring it to your room, with a bowl for water. And, of course you may leave them here, as long as you'd like."

"That's swell. I'd like the Santa Fe. My wife and I stayed in that room a few years ago and loved it."

"It's all yours, Ranger . . . ?"

"Blawcyzk. Jim Blawcyzk."

"Ranger Blawcyzk. Since you've stayed with us previously, you know the bathroom for your room is directly across the hall. There's a bathrobe for your use, hanging on the back of the door to your bedroom. The rate's one hundred dollars for one night, or seventy-five dollars per night for two or more nights. Unfortunately, we don't provide breakfast on weekdays. However, Chrissy's Bakery is just across Bessemer Avenue, a couple of blocks north. She has excellent cakes and pastries. You're more than welcome to purchase some and bring them back here. We do have coffee and other beverages available."

"That's fine. I'll only be here for one night. This isn't exactly a pleasure trip I'm on. In fact, the Hannaford-Smythes are expecting me. Would you let them know I've arrived?"

"I won't need to. They're on the back porch, and asked me to send you out there once you arrived. If you'll just fill out the registration for your room, and make the payment, you can head back there."

"Of course."

Jim filled out the registration slip, then took a credit card from his wallet to pay for his accommodations.

"I hope you enjoy your visit with us, Ranger Blawcyzk," Mary said. "There's no onc at the desk after eight, but your key will also open the front door. Someone will return at seven tomorrow morning."

"I'm sure I will, even if the ghost does pay me a visit," Jim answered, and smiled. "I know where the room is. I'll go see the Earl and Countess before I head upstairs. Thank you."

"You're welcome, Ranger Blawcyzk. And thank you again for staying at the Dabbs."

Jim walked through the dining area and onto the back porch. The Hannaford-Smythes were seated in rockers under a ceiling fan, holding glasses of cold spring water and enjoying the breeze off the Llano River.

"Howdy, folks. Hope I didn't keep you waiting too long."

"We didn't mind waiting at all," Hannaford-Smythe answered. "This place is every bit as delightful as you and the sheriff described."

"And the view from this veranda is just lovely," Mrs. Hannaford-Smythe added. "The river, the old iron bridge, and the water flowing over the dam are all so peaceful. We can hardly wait to begin our explorations."

"We're also absolutely convinced this hotel does indeed have a resident spirit," Hannaford-Smythe said.

"What makes you think so?"

"That dreadful painting of the horrible looking woman, over the stairs," Mrs. Hannaford-Smythe said. "Either she herself is an unfriendly spirit, or she frightened someone to death, and their ghost has been wandering this establishment ever since. Do you know who she was?"

"I'm afraid I don't," Jim answered. "No one around here does. I must say, if she were still alive, she'd be on the top of my list of suspects for whoever killed the person you found. Are you ready for me to finish my questioning? Once I'm done with that, I'm going to take a shower, change clothes, and get something to eat."

"We haven't eaten yet, either, Ranger," Hannaford-Smythe said. "Would it be irregular for us to accompany you to dinner? We really don't have any idea where to find a good restaurant."

"It might be a bit unusual, but I don't see any harm in it. You're not suspects. By the way, where's Stephan?"

"He's in his room. He has a wicked headache, so decided to retire for the evening. If you need to speak with him, I can summon him."

"That won't be necessary. I can always talk to him in the morning, if need be."

Jim turned on his recorder.

"Resuming the interview with Reginald and Olivia Hannaford-Smythe, who discovered the body of the deceased. First, Mr. Hannaford-Smythe, how long have you been in Texas?"

"For close to a month now. We visited Dallas and Fort Worth first, then went down to Austin. We were planning on going straight to San Antonio after that, but the concierge at our hotel in Austin urged us to see more of Texas as it used to be, by exploring the back roads and small towns. She recommended we try the Hill Country first, then work our way south to San Antonio. We were winding our way over to Fredericksburg, Luckenbach, and Boerne, and also to Medina, Kerrville, and Bandera. We took a slight detour when we read about the ghost town of Pontotoc. I must say, if we'd realized what we would discover there, we'd certainly have stayed with our original plans."

"I can't blame you for that," Jim said. "Mrs. Hannaford-Smythe—"

"Olivia. It's so much simpler."

"All right. Olivia, since you were the first person to find the deceased, would you mind telling me again exactly how you did so?"

"Of course. Reginald and I were disappointed to find the walls of the old school in Pontotoc were no longer standing. We decided to rummage through the rubble, thinking perhaps we might find something interesting, possibly some small object we could keep as a memento. While Reginald was poking around the remains of the walls, two old vehicles caught my eye. I decided to look inside them. When I peered into the first one, I saw the corpse."

"What did you do then?"

"I called my husband over. We hurried back to our automobile and called the authorities. Neither of us touched the vehicle containing the corpse, nor disturbed the area."

"Did anyone come out and speak to either of you?"

"No one. We did notice a few people watching us, but we weren't concerned. After all, we do look rather different than most Texans."

"Most Americans, for that matter," Hannaford-Smythe added. "I'm certain most of them were as curious about our automobile as ourselves."

"I can't argue with you there," Jim agreed. "You'll come across expensive vehicles like yours in places like Dallas or Houston. Out here, not so much. Do either of you have anything more to add?"

"I'm afraid not, Ranger," Hannaford-Smythe answered.

"The same for me, unfortunately," his wife said.

"One last question. Would you please give me the name of the hotel where you stayed in Austin?"

"Of course. It was the Westin."

"Thank you. This concludes the interview."

Jim switched off his recorder.

"I'm heading up to my room, to take a quick shower and change into fresh clothes," he said. "If you'd still like to accompany me to supper, we can eat right after that. Have either of you sampled Mexican food, or Tex-Mex, yet?"

"No, I'm embarrassed to say we have not," Hannaford-Smythe admitted, with a shake of his head.

"Then it's high time you did," Jim answered. "There's a little place called Rosita's that serves up fine, real tasty Mexican grub. It's right across the tracks. We can walk there in less than five minutes."

"Excellent. We'll wait right here for you."

"I won't be more than half-an-hour," Jim said. He stood up, started to leave, then turned back.

"Oh, make certain to bring Stephan along," he said, almost as an afterthought. "Some jalapenos or habaneros will clear his sinuses and get rid of that headache."

"He may object," Mrs. Hannaford-Smythe said. "Servants don't usually dine with their masters or mistresses."

"That won't bother anyone in these parts," Jim said. "Bring him. While we're at supper, I'll give you a few suggestions on where to buy some genuine Texas duds. Just make certain you don't get talked into anythin' that makes you look like a pair of Eastern dudes. You want good, plain, working gear, boots and hats, nothing fancy. See you in a bit."

5

As always, Joe Benson arrived at his Llano coffee shop, "Who Spilled the Beans?", just before five A.M. He needed to start brewing coffee for his regular patrons, several of whom would be sitting in their cars in the front lot by six, waiting for him to unlock the doors.

"Now, where in the hell did I put my big French press?" he muttered. "Oh, yeah. I left the damn thing out back after cleaning it last night."

He went to his storeroom. When he flicked on the lights, he stopped short at the sight of the press.

"What the hell?" he exclaimed.

"Yes, indeed. Hell is where you are going. You must die for your transgressions."

"Where are you? *Who* are you?"

Benson looked around for the sound of the voice.

"I am retribution for those who seek vengeance."

The voice was followed by the sound of an engine starting.

Benson froze in horror as his forklift came roaring from behind a rack which held cases of bagged coffee beans. The forks were ten feet off the floor, carrying a pallet stacked with fifty-pound sacks of unroasted beans.

"No. No, don't!" he screamed. He held his hands out, in a futile effort to stop the onrushing machine. It knocked him to the floor, then the operator let the forks drop, the beans crushing Benson as the bags split open.

The operator turned off the forklift and jumped down.

"I guess you know now who spilled the beans," he said. "*I* did."

6

Sheriff Avery and Deputy Kennedy were waiting for Jim when he walked into the coroner's office the next morning.

"Mornin', Jim," Avery said. "Sleep well last night? The ghost didn't disturb you, did it?"

"It might've tried, but I was so worn out I could have slept through World War III," Jim answered. "At least I ate well this morning. The Dabbs doesn't serve breakfast on weekdays, so I stopped at Chrissy's Bakery on the way here to pick up some pastries to tide me over until lunch. Maurice ready to start the autopsies yet?"

"He said in about twenty minutes. He's got to finish sterilizing the room. Hey, did you come up with anything in those old trucks?"

"Maybe some prints, but that's about it. Any DNA that might've been left behind is long gone, thanks to that storm. At least the prints should tell me if we're looking for the same suspect. Deputy, did you start askin' about cock-fighters in the area yet?"

"Last night, I talked to a couple of guys who'd likely be involved, but of course they claimed they didn't know anything about cock fights around here. Oh, they'd heard of some, of course, but they'd never get involved, because cock-fightin's illegal, and they're all law-abiding citizens. I'll keep pressure on 'em."

"The thing I can't figure out is why," Avery said. "What's the motive, especially if the same person did commit both crimes?"

"I haven't got any idea," Jim answered. "Let's hope the autopsies come up with something."

Avery opened his briefcase and pulled out a sheaf of papers.

"Here's the list of people my deputies spoke with, and also the transcripts of their questioning. You can start goin' through them while we're waitin' on Maurice if you wish, but you're not gonna find much."

"I'm obliged for your people's efforts," Jim said. "Might could be I'll want to talk with some of these folks a bit more."

While they waited for the coroner, Jim began reading the transcripts, until Maurice LaPointe came out to the waiting room.

"Good morning. I see you're both here. Ranger Blawcyzk, I've bagged the deceased man's clothing, so when I've concluded the autopsies you may take it for forensics testing. I found nothing in the corpse's pockets, so it appears you didn't overlook anything in your initial search of the body. If you're ready, we can get started."

"We are," Avery said.

"We sure are," Jim added. "There's nothing

quite like an autopsy first thing in the morning to start your day off right."

LaPointe grimaced.

"Well, then, come on in. I decided to do the woman first, because the male's autopsy will be much more difficult."

LaPointe led them down a short corridor, to the morgue. The body of Lillian Gates was lying on a steel gurney, waiting to be autopsied. After all three men had donned protective gowns and masks, the coroner began the autopsy by dictating Gates's name, the county's case number, and the date into his recorder.

"From external evidence, death appears to have been due to asphyxiation by strangling. Deceased was found hanging from a rope in a shed on her property. There are contusions and abrasions around the neck and throat consistent with hanging. The neck does not appear to be broken, with the possible exception of minor fractures, which further examination will confirm. Tongue is swollen and blackened, again consistent with strangulation. Additional scrapings will be taken from under the fingernails to confirm the investigating officer's, Texas Ranger James Blawcyzk, initial findings deceased did not attempt to fend off her possible attacker by scratching or clawing at him or her. There are no other contusions, abrasions, or wounds on the body indicating a struggle. Blood, bodily fluids, and vaginal samples will be taken, to determine presence of any alcohol, narcotics, or other drugs in the deceased's system, or the possibility of sexual assault. I am now proceeding to dissect the deceased's throat, to examine the larynx and trachea."

For the next hour, LaPointe performed the autopsy on Lillian Gates's body. Once he was finished, he rolled the body back to the morgue's main room, and slid it back into its compartment. He removed his gown, mask, and gloves, discarding them into a biohazard trash can.

"I don't know about you gentlemen, but I'd like to take a break before moving on to the next procedure," he said. "I can send my assistant over to Fuel for some coffee and muffins, if you're up for those."

"Sounds good to me," Avery said. "I'll just have my usual. Jim?"

"I could stand a bite to eat. Two corn muffins, plenty of butter, but not toasted or heated. A large coffee, black, no sugar. I guess I'll get my pastries from the truck and have those, too."

"Deputy?" LaPointe said.

"Two slices of wheat toast, strawberry preserves but no butter. Coffee black, with three sugars."

"Fine. I'll be back in a moment."

LaPointe took the money for their snacks from the others, then went to the reception area, returning a few minutes later.

"Amanda will be right back with our food,"

he said. "Ranger Blawcyzk, I'm sorry I couldn't come up with any more evidence for you. Perhaps the toxicology reports will reveal something, but I don't hold out much hope for that. Other than ruling out suicide, I'm afraid my report won't be much help."

"Honestly, I didn't expect much," Jim answered. "Maybe, once I get the items I've gathered back to Austin for testing, the results will show something positive."

"Or with any luck, the corpse from the truck will reveal something," Avery added.

"I doubt it," LaPointe said. "The body is so decomposed it would be a real stretch to think any viable evidence would have remained."

"You mean a real *stretch* of the neck, like on the other body," Jim said, eliciting groans from the others.

"It doesn't matter what we might come up with here," he continued. "I'll be more'n happy just to confirm the same person committed both killings. Unless we get an unexpected break, this case is gonna be one long slog, involving a lot of legwork, and talking to a lot of people, hoping that someone remembers some little thing that will lead us to our killer."

"Have you ruled out Ms. Connors as a possible suspect?" Kennedy asked.

"I hadn't, at least not completely, until the other body was found," Jim answered. "There really wasn't anything suspicious about her actions, and she seemed genuinely grieved over the loss of her wife. I'm still keeping her in the back of my mind as a possibility, but the odds are a thousand to one against her being involved. Deputy, since I'm not as familiar with this county as you are, that's where I'll be depending on you for a lot of the basic grunt work, talking with possible witnesses, seeing if anyone knows a person they think might be involved, places where he or she might be found, all that."

"He's at your disposal for as long as you need him, Jim," Avery said.

"I'm obliged. I've got the use of Ranger Martinez's office until she returns from leave. Deputy, I'll make certain you have any access you need. Just ask. Fred, will the county authorize overtime if needed?"

"The county'll authorize anything you need, Jim. Anything at all. Just so's we catch this son of a bitch."

"Good. Then soon as we're done here we'll get right back to work."

LaPointe was about an hour into the autopsy on the deceased male's corpse when Sheriff Avery's phone rang.

"Sheriff Avery. Yeah?" He paused and held up his hand, signaling to Jim. "Where? How long ago? We're on our way."

He clicked off his phone.

"You're not gonna believe this. That was the Llano Police Department It looks like we've got another one."

"Where?" Jim asked.

"Coffee shop over on East Young Street, not far from here. You can follow me. We'll be there in less than five minutes."

"Let's go."

"Ranger, do you want me to hold up on the rest of this autopsy?" LaPointe asked. "I'm pretty far along, so I'd rather not."

"No, just have your report ready," Jim answered. "Besides, it seems like you'll have a third one to perform. One of us'll call you soon as we're ready to have the body picked up. Fred, let's get rollin'."

The section of East Young Street for two blocks on either side of "Who Spilled the Beans?" was blocked by Llano Police Department units and crime tape. Jim followed Avery and Kennedy as they were waved past the roadblock, and pulled up in front of the small coffee shop. In addition to the police vehicles, a rescue truck, ambulance, and engine from the Llano Volunteer Fire Department were also on scene. The front door to the shop was open, with a portable exhaust fan pulling fumes from the interior. One of the Llano officers, who was carrying an oxygen tank and mask, approached when Jim and the others got out of their vehicles.

"Howdy, Sheriff . . . Deputy," he said, then extended his hand to Jim. "Same to you, Ranger. Lon Haskins, the Llano P.D.'s chief investigator. Also their only investigator."

"Jim Blawcyzk, covering for Ranger Martinez. What have you got here?"

"One dead man, Joe Benson, owner of this shop. Apparently, when his assistant arrived for work, she found the place locked up, with several customers waiting outside. When she unlocked the door, Benson wasn't anywhere in sight, and didn't answer when she called him. She realized the shop was filled with exhaust fumes, so she rushed right back out and called 9-1-1. Soon as a couple of firefighters arrived, they put on their air packs and went inside. They found Benson's body in the storeroom. He was crushed under a pile of coffee beans that apparently fell off a forklift. The lift was still running."

"What happened wasn't an accident, Lon?" Avery asked.

"At first, it appeared to be just that, a freak, tragic accident, Benson somehow getting run over by his own machine, maybe because he'd gotten groggy from carbon monoxide building up. None of the windows or doors were open, so that seemed like the logical explanation. After takin' a look around, however, I'm not so sure."

"What makes you think it wasn't?" Jim asked.

"I only got a quick look around before the fumes got to me, but I saw somethin' that's mighty suspicious," Haskins explained. "Least-wise, I think I did."

"What was it?"

"I'm not real certain, so I'd rather wait until the fire department gives the all clear to go back inside, then I'll show you."

"Guess there's nothin' we can do but wait, Jim," Avery said.

"Guess not, except ask a few questions," Jim answered. "Jody, would you mind asking one of the firefighters how much longer until the building is aired out? Also, locate the assistant and bring her over here. I want to ask her a few questions in the meantime."

"Sure," Kennedy answered. "I know her, name's Laura Webb. I'll find her."

"I left her with Paul Correa, Jody," Haskins said. "She's probably sittin' in his patrol car."

"Obliged, Lon."

While Kennedy went off in search of Webb, Jim asked Haskins a few more questions.

"What can you tell me about Joe Benson?"

"There's not a helluva lot to tell," Haskins answered, with a shrug. "He worked as a cook for a now shut down roadhouse over to Bluffton. He worked hard, and must've saved every penny he could to open this here shop. He's been here in Llano about three or four years now. He got along with pretty much everybody. Went to the Baptist church, and sang in the choir there."

"Family?"

Haskins shook his head.

"None that I know of. He'd been married, but his wife up and left him before he came here. It's my understanding she went back East somewhere. Joe never liked to talk much about her. I'm afraid I don't even know her name."

"I can find out," Jim said. "Did Benson have a falling out with anyone? Was there anyone who might have held a grudge against him?"

"Nobody that I know of. He was just a nice guy, whose life was pretty much his business, and his church."

"But you think someone killed him."

"That's what I think, yeah."

"Can you think of any reason why he might want to kill himself?" Jim continued. "Any financial problems? Did he seem worried, or depressed?"

"Not so's you'd notice. I stopped in for a coffee and doughnut two days ago. He was as cheerful as ever, big smile on his face, passin' along the latest gossip. If someone did kill him, it's a real puzzlement as to why."

"Here's Jody, with Laura Webb and the deputy chief of the F.D.," Avery broke in. "Maybe we'll be able to get inside soon."

"Ranger, this is Deputy Chief Bonnie Arsan, and Laura Webb. Laura was Joe's assistant," Jody said. "Ladies, this is Texas Ranger James Blawcyzk."

"Ladies," Jim said. He bit his tongue to keep from commenting on Arsan's name, which she pronounced 'Arsom'. "I'm sorry we have to meet under such sad circumstances. Ms. Webb, I particularly want to extend my condolences to you."

"Thank you," Webb answered. She was an African-American woman. Jim would estimate her age as about the same as his. She was on the slim side, about five-foot-four. Her hair was cut short, encircled by a colorful headband in the bright red, black, green, and yellow colors symbolizing her ancestors' original homeland.

"I'll need to ask you some questions," Jim continued. "First, Chief, how much longer do I have to wait until I have access to the building?"

"It should be safe to enter in about fifteen minutes," Arsan answered. "The forklift must have been running for quite some time, because the back room was so thick with fumes it was like being in a pea soup fog. There's also no windows back there, so exhausting the bad air is taking a bit longer than usual."

"That's fine. Just don't let anyone touch or move anything you already haven't," Jim said.

"I'll make certain of it."

"I'm obliged. Jody, I'd like you to go back with the chief. I don't want anyone but emergency personnel getting inside that building. Lon, I want you to stay here with me, while I question Ms. Webb."

"Of course."

Jim dictated a new case number into his recorder.

"Ms. Webb, if you are ready, I'd like to proceed with my questioning."

"I believe I'll be able to answer your questions, yes."

"Thank you. I do need to remind you that you are not a suspect at this time. However, you do have the right to refuse to answer any questions, or to stop the questioning at any time. You also have the right to have an attorney present. Do you understand these rights?"

"Yes, I do."

"All right. First, would you please give me your full name and address, for the record?"

"My name is Laura Davida Webb. I reside at 602 Birmingham Avenue, in Llano."

"Telephone?"

"325-499-4809."

"Tell me what happened when you arrived for work this morning."

"When I got here, several customers were waiting. That was unusual, because Joe was never late opening."

"What time was that?"

"I got here just before eight. Mr. Benson always opened at six, but we weren't very busy until after seven-thirty, so he ran the shop alone until then."

"You said he opened at six. What time did he usually arrive?"

"He generally got here by five, to get things ready and start the coffee brewing."

"You are employed as the assistant at Who Spilled the Beans Coffee Shop in Llano?"

"Actually, I became a full partner, half-owner of the shop, just over two weeks ago."

"I see. This was not common knowledge?"

"Not generally, no. The only people privy to the information, besides myself and Joe, um, Mr. Benson, were the loan officers at the Llano National Bank, our attorneys, accountants, and the county clerk."

"Was there a special reason for keeping the information confidential?"

"Not especially. Mr. Benson and I were planning to make an announcement and have a celebration next month."

"All right. Did you ask Mr. Benson for a partnership, or did he offer one to you?"

"He offered it to me. I must say, I was flabbergasted when he did. I'd dreamed of someday owning my own business, but I never imagined it would happen."

"Did Mr. Benson say why he offered you half-ownership?"

"He said it was a reward for all my hard work. That, and he wanted someone who would be as dedicated to the business as he was. He insisted the partnership be set up so if anything happened to either of us, the other person would become sole owner of the business."

"He had no family, nor anyone else, who might have objected to that arrangement?"

"No sir, Ranger. Not that I know of."

"Is it possible he wanted you to invest in the shop because the business was having financial difficulties?"

"Not at all. The shop is doing very well. I had an accountant, and my attorney, go over the books before I agreed to become Joe's partner."

"Ms. Webb, this next question may be a bit awkward, but I have to ask it. Twice now you've called Mr. Benson by his first name. Were the two of you romantically involved?"

Webb grew indignant.

"Hell, no. I mean, of course not. We were good friends, but he's hardly my type. Besides, my boyfriend would kill any man he ever saw flirtin' with me. Everything between me and Mr. Benson was strictly on the up and up."

"I'll need your boyfriend's name, and how to reach him."

"Clarence won't like it."

"I don't care what Clarence likes, or doesn't like. As soon as this interview is concluded, I'll need his contact information, along with the names of your attorney and accountant."

"I've got no choice?"

"None at all."

"You have any more questions?"

"Just two. First, your boyfriend didn't know about your partnership with Mr. Benson?"

"No. That wasn't any of his damn business."

"Last question. Can you think of anyone who might want Mr. Benson dead?"

"No, I damn sure can't."

"That's all for now. Thank you for your cooperation."

Jim turned off his recorder, then pulled a note pad and pen from his shirt pocket.

"I'll need those names now, Ms. Webb."

"Fine. Clarence lives at 519 Vernon Avenue in town. His last name is Sloan."

"His phone number?"

"He's got a Dallas cell phone number, 469-302-4416."

"Your attorney?"

"Jason Conroy, of Conroy and LeMont. You need his address and phone?"

"I can look those up. How about your accountant?"

"Merle Tuttle. You gonna look him up yourself, too?"

"That's correct. I do have to ask you not to leave town, until I've finished my investigation. Here's my card. If you think of anything that might help me find Mr. Benson's killer, if he was indeed murdered, get in touch with me, or the Llano Police. Lon, do you have any questions for Ms. Webb?"

"None that I can think of."

"Fred?"

"Not at the moment."

"All right. Ms. Webb, you're free to leave. However, I do have to ask you not to go near your vehicle until I can search it. You can leave the keys with Deputy Correa. He'll give you a ride home if you need one."

"But you said I wasn't a suspect."

"You're not, but I have to look for any possible evidence. That includes your car."

"Fine. It's a blue Hyundai Accent, parked out back, next to Mr. Benson's Tacoma pickup. You won't find anythin' in it, though."

"As long as I don't, you'll have it back by this evening. Once I'm done searching your car, a Llano police officer will give you a ride back here."

"Thank you."

"Boy, howdy, her attitude sure changed when you asked her if she had a thing goin' with Benson, Jim," Avery said, once the woman was out of earshot.

"You noticed, huh?"

"Couldn't hardly miss it."

"That's for dang certain. Listen, the fire department must have that building aired out by now. Lon, let's go take a look at what you saw."

Deputy Chief Arsan, along with Deputy Kennedy, was waiting at the front entrance to the coffee shop when they reached it.

"I was just coming to get y'all," she said. "Our CO monitors show the concentration of carbon monoxide inside the storeroom has finally dropped to a safe level. Plus, with the fumes cleared out, you'll be able to see more now."

"You haven't moved the body, have you?"

"No, Ranger," Arsan answered. "It was plain the victim was already beyond help, and since this is a suspicious death, we didn't do anything more than absolutely necessary to ventilate the building."

"I'm obliged to you for that," Jim said. "We'll go in now. Jody, you come with us."

Knowing Joe Benson's death had occurred within the last few hours, Jim didn't don his full protective BDU. He simply pulled on two pairs of nitrile gloves, and slid plastic booties over his boots, ordering Avery, Haskins, and Kennedy to do the same.

"Lead the way, Lon," he said, once they were finished.

"Sure, Ranger."

Haskins led them through the main area of the small shop, then through a door and into the storeroom.

"There's Joe's body, right where I found it," he said. "I suppose he might've survived bein' crushed by those damn cases of coffee, but even if he did, the carbon monoxide would've suffocated him."

Jim hunkered alongside Benson's body, to give it a quick look. Benson had been a large man, African-American, probably about six-foot-four and two hundred pounds, in his late thirties to early forties. His black hair was graying at the temples, and over his ears. Dried blood from Benson's mouth, nose, and ears was pooled around his head. One leg was twisted at an awkward angle, the bones protruding. The rest of the body was almost completely covered by the splintered pallet, sacks of coffee, and spilled beans.

"Benson didn't die from asphyxiation," Jim said. "His skin's not cherry red, as you occasionally see in cases of CO poisoning, and his face isn't blue, as it would have been from lack of oxygen. I'd imagine most of his internal organs were crushed, along with several of his ribs, which probably punctured his lungs, perhaps even his stomach, heart, and most of his abdominal organs. I'm guessing his spine was broken, too. He died instantly, or nearly so.

Before I get started, show me why you think this wasn't just an accident, Lon."

"It's right over here."

Haskins led Jim and the sheriff over to the table where Benson had left his French press.

"What the hell is *that?*" Avery exclaimcd.

"That's a coffee press, usually called a French press," Jim answered.

"But what the hell is that in it?"

"That, Fred, is a pressed duck."

The body of a duck, with mostly bluish gray plumage, and white feathers forming a bib down its breast, was jammed into the press, its long neck and head dangling over the top edge of the glass. The press's lid had been placed over the duck's remains.

"A duck? I've never seen a duck that color in my entire life," Avery objected.

"I haven't either," Jim answered. "I'm gonna have to do some research, to come up with its breed. The question is why a dead duck? This case is starting to be for the birds. Good thing I've got room in my office freezer to store the dead fowl for evidence."

He looked around the room.

"We've got a rough day ahead of us. There's gonna be prints from who knows how many persons back here. The firefighters must've left theirs all over the place, too. Plus, when they ventilated the building, they just might've blown out some crucial piece of evidence. On top of that, they moved stuff around. Let's get to work. Lon, I'm assuming you kept the customers that were waiting for Benson to open here."

"I did."

"Good. I'd like you to question them. Also, call the coroner. Tell him he might as well start on over here."

"All right. What do I tell the media when they show up?"

"Don't tell 'em anything, except a suspicious death is being investigated. If they insist on a statement, tell 'em I'll make one after I've finished in here. I'm gonna have to check Benson's vehicle, along with going through Webb's car."

"Not a problem," Haskins said.

"Jody, I want you to dust the shop out front for prints, and look for anything our suspect might've dropped," Jim ordered. "I doubt he, or she, even went out there, but let's not overlook anything. Take photos, too. Fred, you'll stay here with me. Soon as I examine Benson's body, we'll go through this whole place with a fine toothed comb."

"You think it's the same perpetrator in all three killin's?" Avery asked.

"I'm as certain of that as Joe Benson, lyin' there flat as a pancake, is a 'has *bean*'," Jim answered. "Let's get to work."

● ● ●

It was well into the afternoon before Jim finished processing the crime scene. He had found plenty of usable fingerprints, most of which he was certain belonged to Benson, Webb, or the emergency personnel, and several possible sources of DNA traces. Benson's body had been removed by the coroner, and was on its way to the morgue. Deputy Kennedy had accompanied it.

"I guess I'd better call my wife, and let her know I won't be home again tonight," Jim said, as he placed the evidence he'd gathered in the back of his Tahoe. "By the time Benson's autopsy is completed, it'll be late, and I'll be too doggone tired to drive home. I'll spend the night here in town again, then start for Austin first thing in the mornin'."

"Will she be upset?" Avery asked.

"Maybe a little, but she's gotten used to me bein' gone a lot," Jim answered. "Truthfully, I don't know how she puts up with me bein' a Ranger. If things were reversed, I don't know if I could. She's one special woman."

"Then we're both lucky, because my wife's stuck with me for nigh onto twenty years. What?"

Jim's gaze had shifted from Avery to a vehicle parked among those on East Young Street. The Hannaford-Smythe's black Rolls-Royce. A car such as that would stand out anywhere, let alone in a small town like Llano.

117

"I dunno. That's the English folks' Rolls parked over yonder. Now, what the hell would they be doin' here?"

"They probably saw all the excitement, and got curious, so they stopped to find out what was goin' on," Avery said.

"Or maybe, just maybe, there's more to it than that," Jim answered, as he scanned the crowd of bystanders, trying but failing to spot the Hannaford-Smythes, or their chauffeur. "Kinda funny they'd be at two of three murder scenes."

"Well, if you're planning on spending the night at the Dabbs again, you can ask 'em when you see 'em," Avery pointed out.

"I reckon," Jim said. "Hey, before we take off, take a look at this hunk of rock, will you? I've never seen anything like it before."

He handed Avery a baggie, which contained a small piece of stone. The rock was a dark brown granite, shot through with flecks of pink and blue, hexagonal quartz crystals.

Avery instantly recognized the sample.

"This? This is a piece of Llanite. I'm not surprised you've never seen any. The only place on Earth it's found is right here in Llano County, although some geologists claim to have discovered another cache in Brazil. Where'd you find this piece?"

"It was on the floor of the fork lift, right under the clutch. My guess is it was stuck on the bottom of Benson's killer's boot, and fell out when he pressed down on the clutch. What else can you tell me about it?"

"I'm no rock hound, but it's unique enough pretty much everyone around here learns about it. It's a rhyolite, a dark brown granite with those pink and blue crystals you see in it. Some folks call it Que Sera, and claim it has some sort of aura, and gives off some kind of magical powers, or some such nonsense. Personally, I don't buy that crap, but if you come around in March, during the Llano Earth Art Fest, you'll find a whole mess of aging hippies and New Age types who swear it does. It is kind of pretty, though. I got my wife a necklace with a llanite pendant for her last birthday. She loves it."

"Where would an *hombre* be likely to pick up a piece of this stuff, on the bottom of his shoe or boot?"

"There's only one place. It's a road cut on Highway 16, about nine miles north of town. It's a short ways past the Baby Head Cemetery, and just before Ranch 226 cuts back to rejoin 16. There's a pull off in the cut right alongside the highway. The llanite is right there in plain sight, on both sides of the road."

"All right. I'm gonna head out there, and see what I can find. Tell Maurice to go ahead and start the autopsy on Benson's body. I'll meet you at the morgue."

"Right. See you there. Wait. Hold on a minute, Jim. Here comes Lon Haskins. He's got someone with him."

The Llano investigator hurried up. With him was a man of about fifty, with the sun-toughened and wrinkled face of a farmer or rancher.

"Ranger, this here's Marty Comstock. He's got a ranch a few miles east of town. Marty, Ranger Blawcyzk. You already know Sheriff Avery. Tell them what you saw this morning."

"Sure. I was drivin' past Joe's coffee shop about five-thirty this mornin'. I had a load of yearling cows to deliver to the Box G Ranch, over to Grit. Wanted to get that done before the heat of the day. Anyway, an *hombre* ridin' a bicycle come from Joe's lot and cut right in front of me. I had to slam on my brakes to avoid runnin' over him. He was ridin' that bike like a bat outta Hell. Didn't think nothin' of it at the time, although I did cuss him out real good, but when I got back to town and saw all the commotion, I stopped to find out what was goin' on. Once I found out Joe'd been killed, I thought maybe that *hombre* had somethin' to do with it. Figured you fellers would want to know."

"You figured right, Mr. Comstock," Jim said. "Can you give us any description of the man you saw?"

Comstock rubbed his jaw before answering.

"Not a very good one, but I'll do my best. It

120

was still dark, and I really wasn't payin' attention to him, but he got caught in my headlights for just a few seconds. He was a skinny feller, with long hair, went almost halfway down his back. Also had a scruffy-lookin' beard. Had a cap on, that might've been dark gray or black. Wearin' a T-shirt, light colored, and dark pants, probably jeans. He's damn lucky I didn't run him over and squash him flatter'n a June bug under a boot heel."

"That's not a bad description, considerin'," Avery said.

"Mr. Comstock, do you know what color his bike was?" Jim asked.

"I couldn't say for certain, but it looked to be a bright green."

"Mr. Comstock, thank you. You've been a great help," Jim said. "Lon, if you would, take Mr. Comstock's complete statement. Fred, put out a bulletin to all county and local units to stop and question anyone who matches the description. He just might be the man we're lookin' for. I'm gonna head up to that rock formation. I'll still see you back at the morgue."

Jim slowed down as he neared Baby Head Cemetery. To the northeast, the rugged peak of Baby Head Mountain loomed stark and ominous against the skyline. The mountain, and later the cemetery, had been named for a baby girl whose remains, her head impaled on a stake, had been found on the peak, either sometime in the 1850s, or in 1873, depending on which version of the tragedy was being cited. Even to this day in 2019, the mystery of who had killed the infant, and why, was still in dispute. While most accounts claimed the little girl had been carried off and killed by Comanches, another contended the girl's family had been targeted by a conspiracy of rich and powerful ranchers. Those ranchers planned an attack on a family of settlers, to wipe them out, and blame the massacre on the Indians. Their purpose was two-fold: To convince the United States Army to return a cavalry troop to the area, and to discourage more settlers from homesteading in the region.

Once Jim passed the small cemetery, the road climbed a low rise. Jim pulled his Tahoe into the turnout at the summit. The dike of llanite Avery had described was plain to see, jagged, reddish-brown rocks and boulders on both sides of the highway, emerging from the rolling terrain.

Jim got out of his car to search the area around the llanite dike. The ridge was popular with rock collectors, for many scars showed where pieces of the extremely hard llanite had been chiseled off. Smaller shards of rock were strewn about.

"Times like these I wish we didn't have a damn dress code, like the old-time Rangers didn't," Jim muttered, as he loosened his tie. "These cowboy boots I'm wearin' ain't exactly meant for climbing rocks, but I'm feelin' too damn lazy to change 'em."

Jim crossed the highway to look around the dike on the west side of the road first, then returned to the section on the east. He was looking for any rocks showing recent scarring, or perhaps a footprint, or a scrap of cloth, something that might lead him to the person he was looking for. He'd just about given up when he spotted a faint boot print, alongside a large clump of prickly pear.

"Looks like I just got a break," he said. "Gotta go back and get my dental stone."

He returned to the Tahoe, and got his casting kit. Once he returned to the print, he took several photos of it, then knelt down, mixed up the dental stone, and made the cast. Once the stone hardened, he lifted the cast. When Jim stood up, his boot slipped on a sloping rock, and he stumbled slightly. Just as he did, a burning hot pain ripped along his right ribs, a couple of inches below his armpit, followed immediately by the crack of a rifle. Jim yanked his Ruger 1911 from its holster, spinning and dropping to his belly. A second bullet split the air just over him. Jim hugged the rocks, knowing full well if he exposed himself to the hidden gunman the man wouldn't miss again. If he hadn't slipped, the first bullet would have hit him squarely in the middle of his back. With his pistol's range being no match for that of the ambusher's rifle, all he could do was wait the man out. One thing was for certain. Jim had the high ground, and if the would-be killer made any attempt to sneak up on him, or decided to check and make certain he'd killed his quarry, once he got close enough, Jim would put a bullet through his chest, and knock him down for keeps.

Jim's right side was throbbing, sweat mixing with the blood from his wound running down his side. More sweat dripped from his forehead, and plastered his shirt to his back. After ten minutes, he took a chance, lifting his head slightly to look in the direction from which the bullet had come. When no more shots came, he rose to his knees, using the clump of prickly pear for cover. He waited a few more minutes, until certain the gunman had made his getaway. He stood back up and slid his pistol into its holster.

When the bullet hit him, Jim had dropped the cast he'd made. Fortunately, it had landed in the prickly pear, preventing it from falling to the rocks and shattering. Gingerly, Jim reached into the middle of the cactus clump. He was successful in retrieving the cast, albeit at the cost of a good number of prickly pear spines in his hands. Slightly dizzy now, more from the sun beating down on him than the bullet wound, he made his way back to his truck. Once there, he opened the Tahoe's tailgate, and removed his first aid kit. He slammed the gate shut, got into the front passenger seat, turned on the truck's engine, and put the air conditioning on high.

Jim removed his tie and opened his shirt, to expose the blood oozing gash under his right armpit. He gave a sigh of relief.

"This ain't as bad as it feels," he said to himself. "Even though it's bleedin' like a stuck pig, that hole isn't all that deep. I can patch myself up. Won't even need stitches. Should be just fine."

Jim washed out the wound with a bottle of water and antibacterial soap, then dried it and coated it generously with triple antibiotic ointment. After taping a square gauze pad over the slash, Jim took a pair of tweezers and removed the prickly pear spines from his hands. Fortunately, none of those had penetrated deeply under his skin. Removing them now would prevent them from doing so. Lastly, Jim took a few moments to eat several handfuls of cashews, followed by two cans of Dr Pepper.

"That bullet came from the direction of the cemetery," he said, after downing the last of the sodas. "Reckon I'll just mosey on down there and take a look around."

He got out of his truck, rebuttoned his shirt, and slid into the driver's seat. It took less than a minute for him to reach Baby Head Cemetery, and pull up to the gate.

The cemetery was protected by a fence and gate alongside the road, then completely surrounded by a second inner fence, and another gate, neither of which was kept locked. Jim walked through the gates, then stopped a few yards beyond the second fence.

"It'd be real tricky to try and pick off a man up on that rise from down here, but not impossible, especially for an *hombre* with even a halfway decent scope on his gun," he muttered.

Brush, mesquites, and many post oaks covered the ground between the cemetery and the dike. Most of them would have interfered with any ambusher's view of a person atop the rocks.

"I doubt anyone'd try to shoot a man up there from behind any of these trees. More likely he'd hunker down behind one of the tombstones, and take his shot from there. I'll look around the graves first."

Most of the graves in the cemetery dated from the late eighteen-hundreds to the early nineteen-hundreds. Many of the headstones were just thin slabs of limestone or marble, the lettering on many worn away by time and nature. Quite a few had fallen over, lying surrounded by grass and weeds. However, the cemetery was still used on occasion, by long established families in the area who still had plots in Baby Head. Those were marked by thicker, more solid monuments. Jim examined several before he came to the grave of a woman, who had died in 1999, and been buried alongside her deceased husband. There were two impressions in the dried grass, one apparently made by a man's knee, the other by the toe of his boot. There was a fresh scar in the moss and lichen growing on the top edge of the grave-stone.

"Got ya!" Jim exclaimed. "You damned back-shooter. You knelt behind this tombstone for cover, and laid your rifle on it to steady your shot."

He gazed toward the llanite dike. From this spot, the ambusher would have had a clear shot at the unsuspecting Ranger, as Jim was skylined atop the ridge.

"I dunno if the son of a bitch who shot me was smarter'n I am, or I just got dumb and careless. I damn sure never expected anyone to be followin' me, waitin' for a chance to take a pot shot at my back. Wonder if he wasn't careful enough to pick up his shell casings? Could I have that much luck?"

Jim looked around the grave until sunlight glinting off a metallic object caught his eye. He took a pencil out of his shirt pocket, reached down, slid the pencil into a brass cartridge casing, and picked it up.

"Seems like whoever you are, you did get a bit sloppy," Jim muttered. "Hornady 30.06 ELD-X ammo. Guess the Good Lord was lookin' out for me today. If I'd taken this slug in my back, it would've blown a hole clean through me, even from this distance. Lemme see if I can find the other one."

Jim combed through the grass until he found a second casing. He slid the first casing into a baggie, then used the pencil to lift the second one, and placed that one in a separate baggie.

"Now, let's see if I can figure out where you went, *hombre*."

There were a few dim footprints still visible in the grass. Jim was able to follow them to the cemetery's back fence, but they disappeared on the hard-packed ground on the other side.

"No more I can do here, except take a few pictures of the stone the son of a bitch used to steady his rifle. Soon as I take those, I might as well get on into town and see what the autopsies have turned up."

Avery and LaPointe both looked up when Jim walked into the morgue. They stared hard at his torn, bloodstained shirt.

"What the hell happened to you?" Avery exclaimed.

"This."

Jim held up the baggies containing the shell casings.

"Someone took a couple of shots at you?"

"Yup. One of 'em came way too close for

comfort. If I hadn't slipped just when the son of a bitch tried for me, he'd have got me, right in the back." Jim nodded at Benson's naked body, which was still on LaPointe's examining table, partially dissected. "If he had, I'd be the next corpse lyin' on that slab, for Maurice to slice, dice, and julienne."

"Three autopsies in two days is more than enough," LaPointe said. "I don't need you added to the list."

"You mind if I take a look at one of those?" Avery asked.

"Not at all."

Jim handed one of the baggies to Avery. The sheriff whistled while he looked at the casing inside.

"Hornady Precision Hunter. ELD-X, probably .178 grain. This slug could take down an elk at five hundred yards, easy. Whoever pulled the trigger wasn't foolin' around."

"Nope. You can bet your hat he wanted me dead."

"Where'd this happen?" Avery asked.

"Out at the llanite dike. The shooter was down in the Baby Head Cemetery. That's where I found these casings. He left some footprints, but they petered out at the back of the cemetery. I never heard or saw a vehicle, so he must've left on foot. No way to figure where he went."

"Or bicycle, if it's the same *hombre* Marty

Comstock saw," Avery said. "You said the shooter was down in the cemetery?"

"That's right."

"Then he's one helluva shot, to be able to come that close to hittin' you from that far off."

"Actually, Fred, he did hit Ranger Blawcyzk," LaPointe pointed out. "And nearly finished him off. Ranger, you really should have a doctor look at the wound."

"There's no need," Jim answered. "I bled a lot, but it's not all that deep. I patched myself up. Besides, I'll put it in my report, but I'd rather word not get out—at least, not yet."

"Maurice is right, Jim. You need to have that wound treated properly. From the looks of your shirt, you lost an awful lot of blood."

"I'm okay, and I sure don't have the time to waste goin' to an emergency room."

"You don't have to," Avery said. "Obviously, Maurice is a doctor. He can treat you right here."

"In a *morgue?*" Jim exclaimed. "I don't think so."

"Why not?" Avery retorted. "Maurice is as competent a doctor as any. He's finished all three autopsies, so he can go over the results while he works on you. Although I do have a few questions about the shootin', first. So do you let Maurice treat you, or do I call the EMTs?"

"That's blackmail, Fred."

"Damn right it is."

130

"Okay, you win. But if you start to open me up to see what killed me, Doc, I'm outta here."

"All right, I promise to keep away from my scalpel," LaPointe said, with a laugh. "Remove your shirt, then get up on the table. Lie down on your left side."

"*That* table? That's one of your dissecting tables. Not a chance," Jim objected.

"Those are the only tables I have," LaPointe answered. "Don't worry, I sanitized it just this morning. Plus, it hasn't been used for several days."

"I'll have to take your word for it."

Jim pulled off his shirt, hung it over the back of a chair, then got up on the table.

"Damn, that's cold."

"Not as cold as Benson's corpse," LaPointe shot back. "Hold your arm away from your side, so I can get a good look," he ordered.

Jim lifted his right arm, resting his elbow on his head.

"I've got to remove this bandage," LaPointe said. He pulled the tape and gauze off. Jim yelped.

"Yow! Damn, that hurt more than the bullet."

"I'm sorry, Ranger, but some of your armpit hair was stuck under the bandage. It's a good thing the sheriff insisted you have this injury looked at. That hair would most likely have caused an infection. I can also see some bits of injured flesh that need to be removed, or they will also lead to infection. Let me clean out the wound so I can get a better look at it. Oh, by the way, your anti-perspirant and deodorant has failed you."

LaPointe laughed, then turned to take some disinfecting medication, a clean cloth, and bandages from a shelf.

"Jim, let me get my questions out of the way, while Maurice works on you," Avery said. "First, you reckon it was our killer who took that shot at you?"

"That seems to be the most likely scenario," Jim answered. "If it was him, that means he's been watching our every move, leastwise today, probably since yesterday."

"That tells me I should check every piece of video I can find, to see if anyone in the crowd matches the description of the bicyclist Comstock saw at Benson's."

"It wouldn't hurt. One thing that puzzles me is how he knew where I'd be at. He couldn't have gotten there that fast on a bike."

"He probably had a car, or more likely a pickup or van. He had his bike in it. He followed you, either drove past the dike, then doubled back on his bike, or stopped and pulled into the scrub once he saw you'd stopped, then rode his bike to the cemetery. He plugged you, got back on his bike, tossed it in his vehicle, then drove off."

"That makes sense," Jim answered. "Of course, that's not the only possibility. It could've been an *hombre* whom I arrested sometime in the past, and is still holdin' a grudge. He happened to see me in town, saw his chance, and took it. Or even some miserable bastard who just wanted to kill somebody."

"That'd be a mighty long coincidence," Avery objected.

"Ranger, stop squirming, so I can get this done," LaPointe snapped.

"Sorry, Doc. That stuff you're usin' tickles. I've always been mighty ticklish along my ribs."

"Really? Does your wife know that, Jim?" Avery asked.

"She sure does. She touches me in the right spot, and I'm helpless. I'll do anything she asks just to get her to stop."

"Just hold still, Ranger. Unless you want *me* to search for that spot," LaPointe warned, chuckling.

"Okay, okay."

"Jim," Avery continued. "You know, you might've been shot by mistake. It could've been a hunter, who mistook you for a deer, or even a javelina. When he got closer and saw he'd been shootin' at a man, he panicked and ran off."

"Do you really believe that, Fred?"

"No, I damn sure don't."

"Good, 'cause neither do I. As far as we're

133

concerned, from the law's standpoint, until it's proved otherwise, the *hombre* who tried to kill me is the same one who committed the three murders. And once I get the evidence I've collected to the lab, I'll guarantee there'll be some DNA evidence on the shell casings which will match up with some I recovered from the murder scenes. Maybe even, with a lot of luck, some fingerprints that will match."

"Ranger, I'm done cleaning out your wound. I'll give you a choice," LaPointe broke in. "I can suture it, which is what I would recommend, or I can push the edges together, dress and bandage them. Either way, you'll have a scar."

"No needles unless it's absolutely necessary," Jim answered. "Do the best you can without sewin' me back together. While you're finishing up, what did the autopsies reveal?"

"Not much more than you already know, at least not until I receive the toxicology reports. Lillian Gates died of asphyxiation by compression of the trachea and larynx, caused by strangulation by hanging. There were no signs of a struggle. None of the bones in her neck were broken. The unidentified male discovered in Pontotoc died of a broken neck. It's hard to be certain, due to the body's advanced state of decomposition, but my report will show the fracture was clean, just one break. I would testify in court death was almost instantaneous. It appears the murderer is quite powerful, to be able to twist and snap a person's neck like that. Joe Benson died from blunt trauma, crushing weight that fractured his spine, broke almost every one of his ribs, and fractured his skull. Most of his internal organs, including his lungs, heart, liver, spleen, pancreas, and kidneys, were severely damaged, or destroyed, by being compressed and crushed under the heavy sacks of coffee. I'll know whether there were any contributing factors in all three deaths once the toxicology reports come back. I'll have those expedited. Also, I've set Benson's clothing aside in a sealed bag, for you to take to the DPS lab for further testing."

"Pressed duck and pressed coffee shop owner," Jim muttered.

"What'd you just say, Jim?" Avery asked.

"Just thinkin' out loud. Three victims, three dead fowl. And it appears each bird, and the victim it was found with, was killed in the exact same manner. What the hell are we dealin' with here?"

Avery shook his head.

"I don't know, but I'd say if our man had gotten you, I have a hunch there'd be a shot, dead bird with your body, too."

"I'm done here, Ranger," LaPointe said. "You can get down, and put your shirt back on. I assume the bill goes to the state?"

"The only thing this shirt is fit for now is

evidence," Jim said. "I'll get one of my spares out of my truck. After that, I'm gonna grab a quick supper, then head back to the hotel, work up my reports, then get a good night's sleep. I'll be headin' for Austin bright and early. As far as your bill, Doc, yeah, send it along to Austin."

"Unless there's another killin'," Avery said, with a wry shake of his head.

"Let's not even go there," Jim answered. "Folks are gonna be scared enough with the ones we've got. Fred, I'll stop by your office before I leave, to see if Jody has come up with anything."

"All right. The coffee and doughnuts will be on."

Since Jim hadn't eaten since that morning, except for the cashews and Dr Peppers, he was starved.

"I've got a hankerin' for barbeque," he said to himself. "Cooper's and Inman's are both mighty tasty, but Cooper's is just a smidge closer. I reckon I'll go there."

He drove back across the river, and a few minutes later was seated in a booth at Cooper's Old Time Pit Barbeque. He ordered a pound each of brisket and ribs, a baked potato, two sides of cole slaw, and two ears of corn on the cob, all washed down with three extra-large Dr Peppers. He concluded his meal with two pecan cobblers. After eating, he drove back to the Dabbs.

Instead of going upstairs to his room, Jim went

out on the back porch. The Hannaford-Smythes were out there, along with several other guests. Mrs. Hannaford-Smythe waved to Jim.

"Ranger Blawcyzk, how delightful to see you again," she said. "Come, sit and chat with us. Would you like some wine, or perhaps a stronger libation?"

"Thank you, but no," Jim answered, as he sat down. "I just had my supper. I'm also still on duty."

"Well, at least share some of this delightful lemonade," Mrs. Hannaford-Smythe insisted. "It's perfectly chilled, not too tart, and is refreshing on this positively stifling evening."

"Thank you. I reckon I will join you," Jim answered. "Although even if you didn't have your British accents, and we hadn't met before, I'd be able to tell right off you're not from Texas."

"Is that so?" Hannaford-Smythe asked. "How, my good sir, would you be able to do that?"

"Because you're complaining about the hot weather. This is actually a cool spell we're having. I know you're both not used to these kinds of temperatures. Just wait until it gets really hot. It's going to be awfully stuffy in our rooms tonight, since this place isn't air conditioned. This is one time I wish the owners hadn't been so particular about maintaining the historic integrity of the building."

"And the United States still using Fahrenheit makes it seem even hotter," Mrs. Hannaford-Smythe said, as she passed Jim a full glass of lemonade.

"Thank you." Jim took a sip, then put the glass down. "Ah, that is refreshing."

"I would imagine doubly so, after the day you've apparently had, Ranger Blawcyzk," Hannaford-Smythe said.

"It's been one for the books, that's for certain. As long as we're talking about my day, how did you folks happen to be at the crime scene this morning?"

"Purely a case of curiosity. We were on our way to buy some more appropriate clothing, as you suggested. After that, we were planning to explore Enchanted Rock. When we saw quite a few emergency vehicles pass by, going in the opposite direction, we turned around and followed them. I have to confess, the countess and I are both inveterate ambulance and fire apparatus chasers. Is there any particular reason you ask?"

Jim shrugged.

"Not really. Although I would have thought, after what you went through yesterday, with finding the body, then the storm, the last thing you'd want is coming across another murder. Or, perhaps you're both frustrated Agatha Christies."

"We're hardly that," Mrs. Hannaford-Smythe answered. She gave a short, nervous laugh.

"Honestly, we expected to come across a fire, or perhaps an automobile accident. Another murder was the furthest thing from our minds. Although three murders in such a short time is rather fascinating. Quite the mystery, you know."

"How do you know there were three?" Jim asked. "I never mentioned to you there was another murder, previous to the one in Pontotoc."

"From the telly. The story was on all the news programs this evening."

"There's no television at this hotel."

"Yes, that is true. But there is a radio, which the owner keeps set to one of the local stations. The music they play is quite ghastly, but they do have the local news. Also, the hotel does have wi-fi, so we streamed an Austin station for an update."

"Did either of you, or Stephan, leave these premises last night?"

"Are you seriously considering myself and my husband suspects in these horrible crimes?"

"No, but I do have to consider every possibility," Jim answered. "I trust you understand."

"We do, Ranger," Hannaford-Smythe said. "Truthfully, we didn't intend to go anywhere but straight to bed. However, after you went upstairs last night, we decided to go out for a nightcap. We were both feeling restless. We ended up at this really cowboy-style tavern called the Granite-O, I believe. They had one television on an American baseball game, the other on a country music station. You remember, Olivia."

"Of course I do, Reginald. Ranger, we had the most fun, joshing with the cowboys in the establishment. Some of them were so handsome and dashing. Then, the serving girls, particularly one named Eileen. Reginald's eyes nearly fell out of their sockets, he was so busy ogling them, in their low-cut dresses, with their breasts practically falling out. He could barely tear his gaze away from their bosoms the entire time."

"I didn't notice you averting your eyes from those cowboys in their tight jeans," Hannaford-Smythe said, his voice testy.

"No need for anyone to get riled," Jim said. "Looking at pretty gals or good-lookin' guys in a Texas roadhouse is probably the state's second biggest pastime, after high school football on Friday nights. Tell me, was Stephan with you?"

"Stephan?" Mrs. Hannaford-Smythe snorted. "Hardly. He refused to come out of his room. Reginald was forced to take the wheel. Honestly, I'm rather surprised he didn't run off the road on the way back here. He'd had several strong whiskeys."

"Why didn't you drive, then?"

"Me? I wouldn't have even been able to find my way out of the pub's parking lot, let alone back to the hotel. I'd had just as many whiskeys as Reginald. Neither of us is used to such strong libations."

"You might want to remember that next time," Jim scolded. "I'd hate to see you have an accident, and get seriously hurt, or worse. Driving while intoxicated is dangerous enough, but doubly so for you folks. You might forget you're in the States, and start driving on the left, thinking you were back home in the U.K. You wouldn't want to injure or kill an innocent person by driving drunk."

Jim swallowed the last of his lemonade.

"Thank you again for the drink. I've still got some more work to do before I turn in. I have to finish going through some evidence, and writing up my report. I'll be getting an early start in the morning. If I don't see you, have a good time exploring Enchanted Rock. And if you get over to Waco, be sure and visit the Texas Ranger Hall of Fame and Museum. You'll get a real sense of the history of the Rangers. Just give the person at the desk my name and show them my card. Tell them you're my guests."

"Thank you, Ranger," Hannaford-Smythe said. "We'll do just that. Have a good night."

"The same to you both. *Buenas noches.*"

After taking a quick shower and changing into clean clothes, Jim headed back out again. His first stop was at Clarence Sloan's house, a small, run-down metal roofed structure on Vernon Avenue. An old couch, with most of its stuffing torn out, and a pile of haphazardly stacked wood were surrounded by weeds in the overgrown front yard. A yellow, lowered Honda Accord was in the driveway. When Jim knocked at the front door, a dog's deep-throated growl came from inside the house. A moment later, the door was opened by a tall, muscular black man, in his late twenties or early thirties, who stood at least six-foot-six, and probably weighed around two hundred and forty pounds. His head was shaved. He was barefoot, dressed in jeans and a gray T-shirt with its sleeves cut off, revealing arms and shoulders covered with tattoos. He held the dog, a black and white pit bull, by its thick collar, with his left hand. In his right he held a can of beer. He eyed Jim's badge, then glared at him malevolently.

"Yeah? What you want?"

"Clarence Sloan?"

"That's right."

"I'm Texas Ranger James Blawcyzk. Mind if I come in?"

"LuluBelle won't like it."

The pit bull commenced a fierce barking.

"Oh, she won't mind, will ya, girl?" Jim asked the dog. He reached down to scratch her ears. Immediately, the dog stopped barking, sat down, wagged her tail, and licked Jim's hand.

"What the hell?" Clarence said. "Damn, I don't believe it. LuluBelle, what the hell kind of watch dog are you supposed to be?"

"Don't get mad at her," Jim said. "I just naturally have a way with animals. Now, are you gonna let me in? I promise this won't take long. I just have a few questions for you. It might be better if I could ask them inside. I don't imagine you'd want your neighbors gettin' nosy about why a Ranger was at your door."

"You imagine right. C'mon in. Take a seat."

"Obliged."

Once Jim was inside, Sloan closed the door. LuluBelle followed Jim into the living room, sitting on his feet and leaning against his legs when he sat in an overstuffed chair.

"You want a beer, Ranger?" Clarence asked.

"I'd love a cold beer, but no thanks. I'm on duty."

"Suit yourself. You said you had some questions."

"That's right. They concern Joe Benson's murder. Do you mind if I record our interview?"

"I guess not."

"Thank you."

Jim switched on his recorder, had Sloan recite his name and address, advised him of his rights, then began his questioning.

"Mr. Sloan, Laura Webb stated you are her boyfriend. Is that correct?"

"Yes. We've been goin' together for close to three years now."

"How would you describe the relationship?"

"We get along just fine. We both like jazz and the blues, so we spend a lot of time goin' into Austin and visiting the clubs. We also like swimmin' and tubin' in the river. Her place is close to Badu Park, so we spend a lot of time in her backyard, just chillin' with chips and cold beers, watchin' the river roll by."

"I see. So you were both satisfied with the relationship?"

"Sure enough. Just two weeks ago, I gave her a ring, and asked her to marry me. She didn't tell you that?"

"No, but I wouldn't read too much into that, Mr. Sloan. You have to realize, she'd just discovered her employer's body. That would be very traumatic for anyone. In her distress and confusion, it's not surprising she wouldn't think to mention your engagement."

Sloan scowled.

"We're not engaged."

"She said no?"

"Not exactly. She said she needed some time to think about it. Told me to keep the ring until then."

"Mr. Sloan, I don't mean to be rude, and please pardon my sayin' so, but I would think, after nearly three years, Ms. Webb wouldn't need more time to make a decision about her future with you."

"That's what I told her. We had an awful fight.

144

I stormed out of her house, and haven't seen or spoken to her since."

"I am sorry. Is that the first fight you've had, a major one, that is?"

"Yeah, I guess so. We've had arguments before, like all couples, but none like that night."

"Did any of your fights ever become violent?"

Sloan hesitated.

"Mr. Sloan?"

"Yeah, I guess you could say that. But not on my part. I'd never hit a woman."

"But Ms. Webb became violent with you?"

Again, Sloan hesitated.

"You needn't be embarrassed to answer, Mr. Sloan," Jim assured him. "There are battered men, as well as battered women. Anything you tell me here is confidential, unless I need to use your statement for evidence."

"All right. Yes, Laura would hit me when she got mad. Usually, it didn't hurt all that much, since she's so tiny, and I'm a big guy. But a couple of times she gave me a black eye. Then there was the time we were skinny-dippin' in the river. She got mad about somethin', and she held my head under water until I couldn't hold my breath any longer. Later she told me she was just messin' with me."

"That's more than just messing around," Jim said. "That's attempted murder. Any other incidents like that?"

Sloan hesitated once again, before answering.

"Yeah. Laura saw me in the park one night, talkin' with an old girlfriend. There was nothin' to it, we just happened to cross each other's paths. She'd moved on, and so had I. Laura wouldn't hear none of it. She yelled bloody murder, threatened Mata if she ever saw her anywhere near me again, she'd rip her eyes out. Mata was cool. She didn't say a word, just left. Soon as she did, Laura hauled off and kicked me, right in the nuts. She walked off without sayin' another word, just left me lyin' in the dirt, curled up and thinkin' I was gonna die, the pain was so bad. Had trouble walkin' for a week."

"It seems like Ms. Webb has quite a temper. Maybe it's better she wanted time to think about your proposal, Mr. Sloan. Maybe you should give it some more thought, too."

"You're probably right, Ranger. But damn it, despite it all, I love Laura like I've never loved any other woman."

"That, I can understand. I feel the same way about my wife," Jim said. "Funny thing is, Ms. Webb told me *you* were the jealous one. Her exact words were you'd kill any man who tried flirting with her."

"She did? That's a damn lie, Ranger. Listen, I've been in trouble with the law. I ain't gonna hide that. It's all in the records, anyway."

"For what?"

"Stupid stuff. Stealin' a car. Gettin' caught sellin' weed. Never the hard drugs, no meth or crack. No heroin or fentanyl, neither. A couple of drunk and disorderlies. But never for fightin'. And that's all in my past now. I've been clean for nigh onto five years. I've got a steady job as a bulldozer operator for the sand and gravel works here in Llano. The job pays good, and I like it. I'm not about to screw that up."

"I appreciate your honesty. I just have a few more questions. Ms. Webb told me she wasn't romantically involved with Joe Benson. Was she telling me the truth?"

"Laura and that damn fool Benson? I wouldn't be surprised if she had been. She swore up and down their relationship was strictly business. I wanted to believe her, but I sure had my suspicions. That's one reason I asked her to marry me. I thought maybe gettin' married would make her forget that jive turkey."

"Did you know Benson had made her half-owner of the shop?"

"No, I damn for sure didn't. She told you that?"

"She did. Said they were gonna make an announcement in a couple of weeks. You didn't have any hint?"

"No sir, Ranger."

"She stated Mr. Benson offered her the partnership, as a reward for all her hard work."

"Any hard work Laura did for Benson must've

been between the sheets," Sloan answered. "She damn for certain didn't work all that hard behind the counter."

"Mr. Sloan, I apologize for having to put you through this. That's all the questions I have, for the moment. I'll leave my card with you. If you think of anything which might be helpful, get in touch with me, or Investigator Haskins at the Llano Police."

"I'll do that, Ranger. And thank you. You just might've opened my eyes."

"I do have one piece of advice for you. Take some time before you make any decisions. And whatever you do, don't do anything stupid."

"I won't. I give you my word."

"Good. Also, remember that no matter what happens with Ms. Webb, you've already got a good, loyal woman by your side."

"I do?"

"You sure do. Lulubelle."

The pit bull gave a joyful bark. She ran over to Sloan, her tail wagging wildly.

"Don't trouble yourself to get up, Mr. Sloan," Jim said. "I'll see myself out. Good night."

"Good night, Ranger."

Jim shook his head as he closed the door behind him. He was good at reading people. In his line of work, he had to be. And he was positive Clarence Sloan was telling the truth.

"Oh, well, on to the next stop."

Jim opened the Tahoe, slid behind the wheel, and fired it up. It was only a few blocks from Sloan's house to the Granite-O Bar, so he pulled into the parking lot less than five minutes later. The building was a small, squat, windowless structure, its exterior decorated with paintings of deer, turkeys, and other game animals. Several dusty pickup trucks, two with stock trailers attached, were in the lot. Jim backed his Tahoe into a spot near the only door out front, then went inside. About a dozen customers were in the barroom, two of them playing pool, the rest standing at the bar, drinking beer or whiskey. All wore either baseball caps or cowboy hats, denim pants, work shirts, and work or cowboy boots. The room went silent as Jim walked up to the bar. Besides the bartender, there was a buxom woman in her early fifties, her long dark hair pulled back into a thick ponytail, behind the bar.

"Evenin', Ranger," the bartender said. "Anything I can get you? A beer, maybe?"

"Not quite yet. I'm lookin' for some information first."

"Not certain I can help, but I'll tell you what I can. Fire away."

"Did you happen to have a couple of English folks in here last night? Man and woman, both fiftyish, dressed way too fancy for most anyplace in this town?"

"Yeah, they were here. Sure looked different,

and talked funny English, leastwise they said it was English. Real nice folks, though. T'warn't uppity at all. They bought rounds for the house all the while they were here. Said they were tryin' to get a feel for the real Texas."

"I told 'em they'd started at the right place," the woman said.

"You mind givin' me your name, ma'am?"

"Not at all. It's Eileen Willard, otherwise known here at the Granite-O as one hot, spicy mama. That's why the boys gave me this here pin."

She pointed to a pin attached to the left breast of her low-cut blouse. It had an image of a fire and chili peppers painted on it, with the word "Spicy" emblazoned underneath.

"I see," Jim said, with a smile.

"Those folks sure had a fancy car, too, Ranger," one of the men at the bar said.

"That's right, Moe," the man on his left said. "When I first saw it, I thought I'd drunk way too much, since the steerin' wheel was on the wrong side. Figured I was seein' everythin' backwards, 'til ol' Reggie told us he'd had the car shipped all the way over here from England, where they drive on the other side of the road. Sure was a hoot, wasn't it, Johnny?"

"Not as big a hoot as when Livvy tried to learn the Cotton-eyed Joe. She kept getting her feet tangled up. Funniest thing was when she tripped up Larry Pardee, and they both went down, with him landin' on top of her. Larry's wife sure pitched a fit. Too bad he's not here tonight to tell you about it, Ranger."

"I can picture it," Jim said, with another smile. "Bartender, what time did they arrive?"

"Name's Monte, Ranger. I didn't rightly notice what time they showed up, but it had to be around nine-thirty."

"How about when they left?"

"That I can tell you. They stayed until closin' time, midnight. Left after one last drink. Anything else you need to know?"

"Only if you can tell me who might've killed Joe Benson."

"Can't think of a soul," Monte said. "Joe was the salt of the earth. Always had a smile on his face, always ready to lend a hand to folks in need."

"Monte's givin' it to you straight, Ranger," Moe added. "Everyone liked Joe. If any of us here finds the bastard who killed him before the law does, well, let's just say you won't have to worry about a trial."

"Actually, I would. The trial of anyone who decided to take the law into their own hands," Jim answered. "*Comprende*?"

"I reckon."

"If you're finished, Ranger, you ready for a beer now?" Monte asked.

"Just a minute."

Jim removed his badge and put it in his shirt pocket, then pulled off his tie and tucked that in his left hip pocket.

"*Now* I'm ready," he said with a grin. "Long neck Lone Star."

"You've got it, Ranger. Comin' right up."

Jim remained at the Granite-O for nearly two hours, shooting and winning a game of eight ball, talking with the customers, listening to their gossip and mentally noting comments that might be useful in his investigation. When he left, he detoured on the way back to his hotel, to drive by Laura Webb's house on Birmingham Avenue. The home was about the same size as Clarence Sloan's, but in much better condition, freshly painted, with a well-manicured, fenced-in lawn, and pots of colorful flowers on the front steps. No lights were on in the house, and no vehicle parked in the driveway.

"Well, looks like Ms. Webb isn't exactly livin' the high life, but it's not a bad little place she has," Jim muttered. "Wonder where she's got herself to. Seems like I've got to dig into her background a bit more. Wait. Hang on a second."

Jim took out his binoculars, and focused them on a small structure at the rear of Webb's yard, and an object alongside it.

"That's a chicken coop. And next to it's a kid's swimming pool, which has got to be for the ducks I can see sleepin' in the doorway of a doghouse behind it. Well, as Ricky used to say to Lucy, 'Ms. Webb, you've got some 'splainin' to do.' "

He turned the Tahoe around, and drove back to the Dabbs. With the desk clerk long since gone home, he had to let himself in. All the other guests had evidently gone to bed, for there was no one in the dining room or on the back porch. The few lights still on had been dimmed.

"Looks like I'll have the place to myself, so I can work without being interrupted," he said to himself. "Still have a lot to do before I call it a night."

He went into the kitchen, rummaged in the refrigerator and came up with a can of vanilla Coke, then settled at one of the dining tables and opened his laptop.

"Might as well get started."

It was shortly after midnight when the wind picked up. The keys of the old piano on the front porch began jangling. Jim looked up from his laptop and grinned.

"If that's you tryin' to frighten me, ghost, you've gotta do a helluva lot better'n that. Just some of the things I've seen today alone are far scarier than any spook playin' the piano. Give it a rest."

To Jim's surprise, the discordant music stopped.

"Okay, that's better." He turned his attention back to his notes.

Jim worked until after two in the morning, until his eyes grew so tired his vision became blurry. He pushed back his chair, then yawned and stretched.

"I reckon I'd better call it a night. I want to get an early start for Austin come morning."

He shook his head and laughed softly when he realized it already *was* morning. He gathered his files, shut down his laptop, and headed to his room, where he undressed, and put on the bathrobe provided by the hotel. He crossed the hall to take a shower.

Jim was luxuriating under the hot water. He'd just begun washing his hair, which was covered with thick lather, when the lights went out.

"What the hell?" he exclaimed. Shampoo ran into his eyes, temporarily blinding him. By the time he could see again, the lights were back on. The bathroom door was wide open. His bathrobe was nowhere in sight. The sound of someone running down the hall came to his ears, along with an otherworldly, maniacal laugh.

"All right, ghost, ya got me. I'll admit it. I sure hope you didn't wake anyone up. I'd hate to have someone watchin' while I streak for my room."

Jim finished his shower and toweled off. He wrapped a towel around his waist, then peered around the door, to make certain the coast was clear, before stepping into the hall. Once he reached his room, the door slammed shut behind him, before he could close it himself.

"Ghost, I'm too doggone worn out to play your silly games," Jim said. "We'll take this up again some other time."

He dropped face down on his bed, asleep as soon as his head hit the pillow.

7

"We'll be home in just a few minutes, fellers, or I guess I should start callin' you gals," Jim said to the chicks, which were in their box on the passenger seat, as he swung off the I-35 frontage road onto Farm 1626. "It's only a couple more miles."

He had left Llano early that morning, then spent the rest of the day at the D.P.S forensics lab in Austin, comparing evidence from the three murder scenes, studying fingerprints under a microscope. The prints confirmed the killer of all three victims was one and the same person. After Rusty Barclay, one of the chief technicians, assured him testing for DNA would be expedited, due to the urgency of tracking down the killer, Jim spent much of the afternoon at his laptop or on the phone, checking the backgrounds of Lillian Gates and Joe Benson, trying to locate Benson's ex-wife, as well as all the information he could find on Mary Connors, Laura Webb, and Clarence Sloan. On impulse, he had contacted Scotland Yard for information on the Hannaford-Smythes and their chauffeur. Any possible information on the victim found in Pontotoc would have to wait until the man was identified . . . if he ever was.

Just before the spot where 1626 took a sharp

left curve, traffic came to almost a complete stop. A short distance ahead, Jim could see a Travis County deputy sheriff, who was ordering drivers to either detour onto San Leanna Drive, or make a U-turn and head back toward the highway. Jim switched on his strobe lights, passed the vehicles ahead, and pulled up alongside the deputy's car.

"Ranger Blawcyzk, howdy," the deputy said, recognizing Jim. "Sorry for all this."

"Evenin', Terry. What's goin' on?"

"An Austin unit attempted to pull over a vehicle without a license plate. Idiot drivin' it didn't stop until he was blocked in by another Austin officer. Turns out the driver claims he's one of those sovereign citizens, who thinks the laws don't apply to him. He's refusing to get out of his vehicle until a supervisor shows up. Damn fool's wastin' everybody's time, and for what? He's gonna end up bein' arrested and tossed in a cell, instead of just gettin' a traffic ticket."

"How long has this been goin' on?"

"A little more'n forty-five minutes now."

"Then it's time to end it. I'll take care of the problem."

"I was hopin' you'd say that, Ranger."

"After the few days I've just had, it'll be a pure pleasure to straighten this fool out."

"Good luck."

Jim waved as he drove off. At another curve in the road, a newer model Ford Fusion was blocked in by two Austin police units, with another Travis County deputy's vehicle parked blocking the left lane. Jim stopped his Tahoe behind that unit.

The two Austin officers, along with the deputy, were standing grouped near the driver's door of the Fusion.

"Good evenin', gentlemen," Jim said, as he walked up. "What's the situation here?"

"The bastard inside this here car states he's a sovereign citizen, answerable only to common law, Ranger," one of the Austin officers answered. "He's refusing to provide any identification, nor open his window. All of us have explained to him several times he has to comply, but he insists on speaking to a supervisor, in person."

"I'll handle the son of a bitch," Jim said. "It won't take but a few minutes."

He went to the back of his truck and removed his shotgun, then walked up to the Fusion. He stood alongside the driver's window, which was opened slightly. The driver, a man in his early thirties, wearing a reversed baseball cap over longish sandy hair, looked at Jim, then held his phone against the window, apparently recording the encounter.

"Sir, I understand you are refusing to produce your license, registration, and insurance information to these officers, nor any form of identification, as required by State of Texas motor vehicle statutes."

"They have no right to any of that information. I am a sovereign citizen, subject only to common law, and the law of God. I have committed no crime, so they have no right to stop me. Are you their supervisor?"

"No, sir, I'm a Texas Ranger. My authority in the state of Texas supersedes that of any local, county or other state law enforcement officer. Now, are you going to comply with the officers' request?"

"I want your badge number and name, Ranger. I also advise you I am recording this."

"Rangers don't have badge numbers. My name is not germane to this situation, so I don't have to provide it to you. We also don't play games with lawbreakers, so I'll only ask you one last time, will you give the officers your identification?"

"No, Ranger, I will not. I am not driving a commercial vehicle. I am traveling in a private conveyance, not driving. Therefore, I am not required to have a driver's license, nor a Texas registration. The plate on my conveyance which says 'Citizen' explains that. I have committed no crime."

"You have committed several traffic violations, according to the officers, and refusing to provide proper identification *is* a crime. Now, please step out of the vehicle."

"No, Ranger. You have no right to demand I do so."

"You have ten seconds."

The driver sat silently while Jim counted down the ten seconds.

"You were warned, sir."

Jim reversed his shotgun, and used the butt to smash out the window. He pulled his knife from its sheath, reached into the car, unlocked and opened the door, then sliced the seatbelt in two, while the driver screamed and cursed. Jim dragged him from his car and shoved him against the back door.

"He's all yours. Go ahead and cuff him," Jim said to the deputy and Austin officers. "Now *that's* how you handle one of these so-called sovereign citizens. There's no point in wastin' time on 'em, just arrest 'em and put their sorry butts in jail, so the courts can handle 'em. Now, I'm goin' home. I've had three long, hard days, and the ones ahead promise to be the same. You know how to reach me if you need to. Oh, I guess you can cancel your supervisor."

"I reckon we can at that," the deputy said, chuckling. "G'night, Ranger. And thanks. We're obliged."

"Anytime. G'night."

Kim, Josh, Jim's mother Betty, and Frostie were on the screened-in back patio when Jim pulled up. The new neighbors, Porter and Babs Howfield, were with them, along with the Howfields' two children, twelve-year-old Patricia and nine-year-old Jacob. Copper, Jim's sorrel and white paint gelding, whinnied a greeting from his corral when he saw Jim get out of his truck, then went back to nibbling on hay.

"Somethin' sure smells good," Jim said, as the odor of grilling meat came to him. "I'm more'n ready for a home cooked meal."

Frostie came bounding up to Jim, then followed him to the patio, walking on his hind legs while he sniffed at the box holding the chicks.

"Howdy, folks," Jim said, nodding to the Howfields. He sat in the empty chair alongside Kim and kissed her on the cheek.

"Boy, howdy, am I glad to be home, at least for one night." he said. "I've sure missed you, honey. You too, Ma. And I've really missed you, little pard," he continued, when Josh crawled up to him. He put down the box holding the chicks, picked up Josh, kissed him, and held him in his lap. Frostie began pawing frantically at the box.

"We're all glad to see you too, Jim, but what in the world is in that box?" Kim answered. "Whatever it is, it's driving Frostie crazy."

"It's a present the Llano County sheriff bought me, and I'm gonna give to you. Frostie, give it a rest!"

Jim took the box and handed it to Kim.

"Go ahead, open it."

161

"I'm not certain I should."

Tentatively, Kim opened the box.

"Jim! More chicks. Why? You thought we already had too many."

"Ah, but these are special. They're Speckled Ranger chicks, or Speckledys. That's why the sheriff got 'em for me. They're also evidence in one of the cases I'm working on."

"Jim, I don't know if we have enough room in the coop for two more hens," Betty said.

"That won't be a problem, Ma. They can stay in the horse barn until they're a bit larger, then join the flock. They're good free-ranging birds, so they'll only need to stay inside when it's time to roost for the night, or if the weather's real bad. I'll take them there now."

"I'll do that," Betty said. "You just stay here and take it easy. You look tired."

"I sort of am," Jim answered. "What's on the grill? It sure smells good."

"I'm trying out a new recipe for barbeque sauce, so I'm doing chicken," Kim said.

"Kim! Not in front of the chicks! We don't want them to know we're eating their relatives. They'll think we're cannibals."

"Jim . . . Oh, never mind," Betty said. "Just give me those chicks. I'll be right back. There's beer and Dr Pepper in the cooler. Iced tea, too."

"May we see the chicks, Mrs. Blawcyzk?" Patricia asked.

"Of course you may, sweetie," Betty answered. "Why don't you and your brother come with me? You can help me settle them in their new home."

"May we, Mom?" Jacob asked.

"I'm not certain it's safe," Babs answered. "You might get trampled or bitten by one of the horses. And you know you have allergies."

"They'll be fine," Jim assured her. "The horses are in their corrals, and the doors to their stalls are closed. There's nothing to worry about."

"Porter, what do you think?" his wife asked.

"Just this once."

"All right, go ahead. But make certain you listen to Mrs. Blawcyzk. Jacob, if your eyes start to water, you get stuffed up, or you break out in hives, come straight back here."

"All right, Mom. Thanks."

"Patricia, Jake, let's go," Betty said with a smile, the box in her hand. They started for the barn.

Jim took a can of beer from the cooler, opened it, and took a long swallow.

"Man, that tasted good."

"Jim, are you certain the children will be safe?" Porter asked.

"Of course they will be. I know this isn't exactly Briarcliff Manor, where you folks hail from, but it ain't the Wild West, either. In fact, Dallas, nowadays, is pretty much New York City, only with cowboy hats and boots. Same goes for

Austin. We've got plenty of culture here in Texas, just like New York. You simply have to know where to find it."

"It's just so different here than back home," Babs said. "However, when my company offered me the C.E.O. position of their largest division, I couldn't turn it down, especially when Porter was also able to transfer to Austin."

"Things aren't all that different, except the weather," Kim said. "You'll find most people are probably friendlier than back East, and you have so much to explore. New cuisine, new places, new activities. Plus, you just built a beautiful new home."

"It simply doesn't feel like we belong yet," Babs said. "Of course, we were very fortunate to find Consuela for a housekeeper and nanny. The children both adore her."

"There you go," Jim said. "Consuela can teach your kids a lot about the history of Mexicans and Latinos in Texas. Their history goes back far longer than us Anglos. Patty and Jake will learn Spanish far more easily from Consuela than in any classroom, tryin' to memorize words out of a textbook. She'll also show you how to create Tex-Mex dishes, too. You've already made a good start by hiring her. Listen, if y'all will excuse me for a minute, I'm goin' to change out of these clothes. It's high time I lose this tie and dress shirt. Be right back."

• • •

Jim came back outside a few minutes later, now dressed in a Company F T-shirt, jeans, an old, dirt and sweat-stained Stetson, and well-worn, scuffed boots. Instead of his service pistol, he now wore around his waist a gunbelt and holster which carried an antique, but still working, .45 Colt Army SAA "Peacemaker" revolver, the same six-shooter which the first James Blawcyzk to serve as a Texas Ranger had worn, back in the 1870s.

"I didn't take too long, did I?" he asked. "Sorry if that was a bit rude, but I needed to get into an outfit I can relax in."

"No, you didn't at all," Kim said. "The chicken still has to cook for another fifteen minutes or so."

"I have to say, Jim, having the gunbelt around your waist certainly doesn't look all that comfortable," Porter said.

"It just doesn't feel right *not* havin' a gun on my hip," Jim answered. "Besides, since I'm on call 24/7, I'm always armed. Have to be. Sometimes you might not be able to tell, but I've always got a firearm on me somewhere."

"That's enough talk of work, of any kind, from all of you," Kim ordered. "There are many more pleasant topics to discuss. And here comes Betty and your children, Porter."

"Mom, Dad, those chicks are so cute. Can we

get some chickens, please?" Patricia pleaded, as she ran onto the patio.

"Of course not. It's out of the question. Your father and I certainly don't have time to care for chickens, or any other pets. And don't forget your brother's allergies. It's impossible."

"But Mom, I didn't sneeze, or have any trouble breathing, all the while we were with the chickens," Jacob said. "We even petted Mr. Blawcyzk's horse on his nose, when he came into the barn and neighed at us. He even licked our hands."

"Sounds like Copper's figured out how to open his gate again, Jim," Kim said.

"Seems so," Jim answered.

"You touched a horse?" Babs echoed Jacob, horrified.

"We sure did," Patricia said. "His nose is so soft, like a pillow."

"Babs, I apologize," Betty said, trying to mollify the indignant mother. "I told them they needed to ask your permission first, before getting near any of our horses, but they ran right up to Copper before I could stop them. That horse loves people, and Jim has him spoiled, so he expects everyone to pet him or feed him treats. Plus, Copper's too dang smart for his own good."

"It's not your fault, Betty," Porter answered. "All children have a natural fascination with animals. Your horses are merely an attractive nui-

166

sance, that's all. Perhaps you could keep them more confined, at the least, a bit farther back from our property line."

Kim gave Jim a warning look, sensing her usually easy-going husband was about to explode. Anyone complaining about or bothering his horses always brought out that reaction. She broke in before he could speak.

"I'm sorry; however, I'm afraid that wouldn't be practical, Porter. Horses don't do well confined in a stall most of the day. They need to be out where they can graze, run, and stretch their legs."

"But our children's safety . . ."

"Your kids'll be fine, as long as they know how to act around horses," Jim said. "No, let me finish, Kim. Porter, Babs, I realize you're both from back East, so you might not quite understand many things about Texas. Horses are a part of our heritage, as much as cattle, oil, and farming, and many other things, including guns. I'm not trying to tell you how to raise your kids, but havin' a few hens around your place might not be a bad idea. Hens are easy to care for, don't come in the house, and for a bit of feed, and letting them wander around, pecking at insects, which will help keep the bug population on your property down, they'll provide you with fresh eggs. Taking care of the chickens would also help teach Patty and Jake responsibility. As far as our horses, any of us'd be more'n happy to teach your kids how to brush and care for them, and how to ride."

"See, Mom, Dad—I'll bet Consuela would like to have chickens, too," Patricia said. "And you always promised I could take riding lessons."

"Could we get a dog, too?" Jacob added. "I've always wanted one. All I have now is my aquarium. I mean, I like my fish, but I can't hold them, or pet them."

"I won't have a dog in my house, to leave hair everywhere. I don't want the mess."

"You don't have to, Babs," Kim answered. "You have enough room for a dog that would be happy outside. There are many, many dogs in shelters, waiting for a forever home. A dog run, with a house in the shade for protection from the sun and heat, would be perfect, certainly far better than waiting in a shelter for a family that never comes. Or being there so long the poor animal gets put to sleep. Alternatively, there are quite a few breeds which hardly shed, and are small, so even people with allergies can usually own one of those dogs."

"Not to mention, a dog is mighty good protection against intruders," Jim added. "Even one like Frostie, who loves just about anyone, unless they come into our house before he gets to know 'em. A dog that barks is usually enough to scare off any would-be burglar."

"But Jacob has those allergies," Babs objected.

168

"And our house has the best security system available."

"We've also got you for protection, Jim," Porter added. "I would imagine having a Texas Ranger for a neighbor would be a most powerful deterrent."

"Except I'm not here all the time," Jim answered. "Also, I hate to tell you this, but no one has yet come up with a foolproof security system, that'll stop a determined intruder."

"That's for certain," Betty said.

"As far as your son's allergies, there's usually a solution for those," Kim answered. "I had them also, but my allergist came up with a holistic treatment program that has practically eliminated my reaction to animal hair and dander. That's greatly changed my life. I even brush my horse with no problem. I can refer you to her if you'd like."

"Yeah, Mom, that's a good idea," Patricia said. "You know me and Jacob have always wanted a dog, and a cat. Please."

"Jacob and I, darling. I'm still not certain having pets is a good idea. What do you think, Porter?"

"I'm not certain either, but Jim does have a good point about the children learning to be responsible, and a dog would be protection for the children while you and I are working. Perhaps we could think about it."

"See, Mom. We'll learn a lot by having pets," Patricia said.

"Patricia, Jacob, I merely said your mother and I would give the matter some thought. We're not making any promises. Before any decision is made, we'd need to consult with Consuela, to see if she would be willing to have animals to look after, along with you two. Your mother and I will have to talk this over, first."

"Aw, gee," Jacob moaned.

"That's enough, Jacob."

"Porter, do you mind if I say something?" Jim asked.

"No, go right ahead."

"Okay, here goes. I'm gonna be honest. When I first heard you folks were from New York, and then saw the fancy house y'all were buildin', I wasn't certain what kind of neighbors you'd be. I thought maybe you'd think you were too high-falutin' to associate with the likes of me, an old-time Texas lawman. But once I met y'all, you turned out to be real nice folks."

"We appreciate that, Jim. We're happy to have you and your family as neighbors, and, I hope, friends, for a long time."

"Same for us. What I want to say is this. Now that you're Texans, well, at least working on that, to start fittin' in, you need to be a little less New York and a little more Texas."

"What exactly do you mean?" Babs asked.

"You need to loosen up a bit. Get into the swing of things. For example, instead of those polo shirts with the little alligator on 'em you always wear, Porter, get yourself some T-shirts. Trade in those khakis for jeans when you're not at work. Get yourself a good pair of hand-made cowboy boots to wear at the office. Those are pretty much *de rigeur* footwear for every executive in every boardroom in Austin, Dallas, or Houston. Buy yourself a good Stetson, too. I noticed you always call your kids by their full names. That won't do down here. Call 'em Patty, and Jake. Take your wife to an Austin honkytonk. Learn how to do the Texas two-step, and Cotton-eyed Joe. Then, the next week, y'all can take in a symphony, play, or the opera, if that's what you want. You can do all the fancy stuff you'd like, but if you try to act high-toned and sophisticated all the time, you'll never truly be Texans. And get the kids that dog, and the chickens. Let 'em learn how to ride a horse, too."

"What my son is so clumsily trying to say, Babs, is have some fun, and put a little spice into your lives," Betty said. "Break out of your mold, and try something new. In fact, I just had an idea. Kim and I will take you shopping. We'll help you pick out some new outfits. We'll have you dressed like a Texas woman before you know it. An empowered, smart, confident boss lady Texas woman."

"Speaking of spicing up all our lives, the chicken should be done," Kim said. "The new sauce I'm trying is loaded with jalapenos and habaneros. I'm not certain exactly how hot it will be, but it's bound to be blazing. Grab your plates."

It was now a little past ten o'clock. The Howfields had gone home, with plenty of leftovers. Josh was asleep in his crib. Jim, his wife, and mother were sitting in the living room.

"Jim, I didn't want to bring this up while our guests were here, but of course I've been following the stories about those murders, on the news," Kim said. "I realize you can't divulge much, but have you got any idea who might be responsible?"

"Not yet. I know it's the same person, from the fingerprints, and I'm awaiting the DNA results, which should tell me more about him."

"Or her," Betty said.

"That's possible, but from the evidence I've gathered, I'm almost certain the suspect is a man. In fact, perhaps you and Kim can help me with one piece of evidence. Would you mind taking a look at a photo if I show it to you? I'd be obliged."

"Not at all."

"I do have to warn you both, it's pretty gruesome."

"Now, *there's* a surprise," Kim answered. "As

172

if you've never shown us ghastly crime scene photos before."

"I reckon you have a point."

Jim got his camera and scrolled to the photo he wanted, the badly decomposed carcass of the chicken found in the abandoned pickup in Pontotoc. He handed the camera to Kim.

"I need to know what breed of chicken this is, if you can possibly tell me. Even an educated guess would help. I know there's not much of it left to work with."

Kim studied the photograph for a moment, then handed it to Betty.

"I'm pretty certain I know what breed this is, but I'd like to get your thoughts before I say," she said.

Betty needed only a brief glance.

"That's a white leghorn."

"That's what I thought, too."

"You're both certain?" Jim asked.

"Yes," Kim answered. "The size of the bird, and its white feathers, give its breed away."

"Thanks, both of you. That saves me from a trip to the state's forensics veterinarian. Look, I hate to cut the evening short, but I have to be back in Llano first thing in the morning, so I'm gonna call it a night."

"I was just about to say it's time for me to get home," Betty said. "After all, it's such a far way to go."

"Yeah, at least a five-minute walk," Jim said, laughing.

Jim's mother lived in a small house, with an attached studio where she made stained glass suncatchers and windows, which Jim had built for her after the death of his father. It was situated on the northwest corner of the Blawcyzk homestead.

"A bit longer, if I do some star-gazing," Betty answered. "You two needn't get up. Kim, I'll see you in the morning. Good night."

"Good night, Betty."

"Night, Ma. I'll be gone before you get here," Jim said.

"As usual," Betty answered.

"Time to get some sleep," Jim said, once he heard his mother close the door. He started laughing.

"Getting sleep, that I'm certain you need badly, is funny, Jim?" Kim asked.

"No, not at all. The look on Porter's face when he took the first bite of his chicken just crossed my mind, that's all. I've never seen an *hombre*'s face turn that shade of red before. I was beginning to think he was gonna drink our well dry before he finished."

"Well, I did warn everyone the sauce might be hot, a trifle."

"And it was, a trifle," Jim answered. "Babs certainly took it in stride, though. She never even sucked in a deep breath."

"She did gulp down a long neck awfully quick, though."

"Shows she's got what it takes to be a Texas woman," Jim answered. "I'll bet the kids get their dog, too."

"I'm not so certain. Would you care to make a small wager, husband dear?"

"Sure. What's the prize?"

"If you win, then you get a night of dining and dancing at Austin Jack's Roadhouse."

"And if you win?"

"Dinner at Chez Français, and a show."

"Afterwards?"

"Afterwards, we both win."

"You're on. I say within a month the Howfield kids have a dog."

"And I say not a chance. It's a bet. Now, let's go to bed."

"I thought you'd never ask."

8

Nguyen Tranh had made his final delivery of the day, to the H-E-B store in Kingsland, thirty minutes earlier. He ran a one-person wholesale business, delivering specialty Asian meats and vegetables to stores and restaurants in both Llano and Burnet counties, as well as several bars and nightclubs in Austin. He had returned to his warehouse, where he was hosing out his refrigerated delivery truck.

Nguyen was washing down the cargo compartment's front wall, so he had his back to the open rear doors. He turned at the sound of someone scrambling into the truck. He stood, puzzled, at the sight of a man standing there, holding a chicken. For some reason, the bird hadn't cackled.

"Sir, what are you doing here? May I help you?" Nguyen asked.

"You certainly can." The man's right hand had been hidden behind his back. He now brought it into sight, revealing the razor-sharp machete he held.

Terrified now, Nguyen dropped the hose, and backed into the compartment's right front corner. He lapsed into his native Vietnamese, pleading for mercy. His assailant merely gave a grim smile, swung the machete, and cleanly severed Nguyen's head from his body. Limbs still writhing, Nguyen's body dropped to the floor, his head rolling into the opposite corner.

"Now, Trudy, it's time for your contribution to our quest."

The chicken's owner sliced off her head, then tossed her carcass against Nguyen's body. He jumped out of the truck, shut the back doors, and casually strolled away.

9

Jim's first stop in Llano the next morning was at the home of Stacy Martinez, the Ranger who normally covered Llano County.

"Good morning, Stacy," he said, when she answered the door. "I appreciate your takin' the time to see me."

"It's not a problem at all," Stacy answered. "C'mon into the kitchen. I've just put Melinda down for her morning nap. Mike's already gone to work."

Jim followed Stacy to the kitchen, where her newborn baby girl was sleeping in a small bassinet.

"Stacy, your baby is so doggone cute!" he exclaimed. "She looks just like you."

"*Gracias*. My mother says the same thing. But Mike's says Melinda looks just like him."

"That sure sounds like grandmas," Jim said.

"Have a seat, Jim, while I get you a cup of coffee. Black, like always?"

"You've got it right."

Stacy poured two cups full, handed one to Jim, then sat down across from him.

"Go ahead, Jim. You've got some questions about the recent murders."

It was a statement, not a question.

"That's right. I was hopin' maybe you could shed some light on 'em. Do you have any idea who could possibly be pullin' those killings off?"

"I wish I did. In fact, honestly, I wish I was back to work, and handling those myself," Stacy answered. "I know you've got more details than have been released to the public."

"That's right. Three victims, one female, lesbian; one apparently Hispanic; the third, a black male. First one ran a small farm with her wife; only clue I have about the second is a cockfightin' spur found with the body; and the third ran a small coffee shop. No connections between any of 'em, as far as I can tell, except both the first victim and the third were growin' marijuana. One dead chicken at each of the first scenes, a dead duck at the third. I've got no idea on a motive. Each bird appears to have been killed in the same manner as the person with which it was found. That's one detail which hasn't been released to the public yet."

"What about the Hispanic male? Any drugs on him, or in his system?"

"None on him. His body was so badly decomposed I still can't be certain he even *was* Hispanic. It was so far gone, I doubt even dental records would be any help. Unless someone has, or does, turn in a missing person's report, and a DNA sample for a match, he'll likely never be identified. I'm still waitin' on the toxicology reports to see if any of 'em had taken any drugs. I'm hoping you can give me some information about the victims, or perhaps an idea of who might be responsible."

"I'll try, but I'm afraid I won't be much help. I didn't know Lillian Gates at all. I only stopped in Joe Benson's shop a couple of times. His stuff was too expensive, and I didn't care for all the fancy lattes and mattes and mocha this's and cappuccino frappe that's he sold. When I want coffee, that's all I want—*coffee*."

Jim laughed.

"Yeah, you're about the only person I know who likes her coffee as strong as I like mine. Lieutenant Stoker has told me more'n once you brew coffee almost as bad as I do."

"He's a big baby when it comes to coffee."

"Agreed. How about who might be the person committin' the murders? The evidence shows it's the same man, or woman, although I have a strong hunch our suspect is male. I've got a half-way decent eyewitness description of an *hombre* ridin' a bicycle leaving Benson's shop about the time the murder took place. White male, skinny, long hair and beard. The witness thinks the bike was green. Also, here's a bit of news. Laura Webb was just made a full partner in Benson's shop a couple of weeks back. I reckon she's now sole owner. Clarence Sloan, her boyfriend, thinks she and Benson were more than just business partners. Said he asked her to marry him, hopin' she'd maybe give up Benson, but she told him she needed to think about it. Webb told me Benson wasn't her type, and that Sloan was the jealous type, who'd kill any man who even looked at her. Sloan told me just the opposite, that Webb had even beaten him up, more'n once. But he says he still loves her."

Stacy shook her head.

"Poor Clarence."

"What d'ya mean by that?"

"That boy can never catch a break. His mother was a drunk, his father a no-good gambler, who beat both his wife and the boy. He was stabbed to death during an argument over a dice game. Clarence had plenty of scrapes with the law, but he'd finally gotten himself a good job. Things seemed to be comin' around for him. Now, this."

"You believe him, not her?"

"I sure do."

"How about Webb and Benson? Anything there?"

"I wouldn't doubt it. Jim, you talked with both Webb and Clarence. Which one would you say was tellin' the truth?"

"If I had to testify to it in a courtroom, I'd say Sloan."

"And you'd be right. Laura Webb is a nasty little *bruja*."

"I can believe it. What about the *hombre* on the bike?"

"That describes an awful lot of people in Austin, but damn for certain not in Llano. There's a few, so you shouldn't have too much trouble finding and questioning them. You might want to have your witness go through the photos from last year's LEAF festival. He might recognize someone."

"That's a good idea. Sheriff Avery assigned Deputy Jody Kennedy to assist me. I'll have him round up our witness and do that."

"Jim, could I ask you a favor?"

"As long as it doesn't involve changin' Melinda's diapers, sure."

Now it was Stacy's turn to laugh.

"I promise you, it doesn't. I'd just like you to keep me abreast of any developments. I'm about to go stir crazy, being stuck here at home."

"Even with the baby?"

"Yes. I love her dearly, but I have to work. You understand."

"I sure do. And, of course, I'll keep you up to speed."

"Would I be able to convince you to leave me copies of all your files?"

"I'm not the one you have to convince. Get Major Voitek's permission, and I'll be glad to."

"I'll get on the phone with him as soon as you leave. What's your next move?"

"Lots of legwork, and diggin'. You know how that is."

"I sure do. That's always . . ."

Jim's phone rang.

"Hold on a minute, Stacy."

Jim answered the phone, and put it on speaker.

"Ranger Blawcyzk."

"Ranger Blawcyzk, this is the Llano County Sheriff's Department. Sheriff Avery would like you to meet him at the Llano News. That's at 813 Berry Street. They've received a communication which may be relevant to the recent murders."

"Tell the sheriff I'll be there in about ten minutes."

"Yessir, Ranger."

Jim clicked off his phone.

"I've gotta run, Stacy. With any luck, this will be the break I need."

"I sure hope so. Keep me posted."

"Will do."

Sheriff Avery's vehicle was parked in front of *The Llano News* office, a storefront in a row of old brick, one- and two-story buildings. A Llano police officer was standing in the adjacent space, evidently holding it for Jim. He stepped aside when he saw Jim pull up.

"Sheriff's waitin' for you inside, along with Lon Haskins, Ranger," the officer said, once Jim got out of his Tahoe.

"Thanks, officer. I'm obliged to you for holdin' the parkin' space for me."

"*De nada.*"

When Jim went into the newspaper's office, Sheriff Avery and Lon Haskins were seated next to one of the desks, behind which sat a woman in her early thirties. She stood up when Jim approached. A reporter whom Jim recognized was seated at the desk behind hers. Jim nodded to her.

"Jim, this is Toni Leavitt, editor of *The Llano News.* Toni, Ranger Jim Blawcyzk."

"I'm pleased to meet you, Ranger Blawcyzk," Leavitt said.

"Same here, Ms. Leavitt. I understand you have received something, which may be connected to the recent string of murders in the area."

"That's correct. We received a letter in this morning's mail, addressed to Bonnie Tyson, the reporter who has been covering the story. You've already spoken with her previously."

"I have."

"Bonnie, tell Ranger Blawcyzk exactly what happened this morning," Haskins told the young woman behind Leavitt.

"Of course. When the mail was delivered, I took it, and began sorting through it, as I do every day. There wasn't much, a couple of subscription payments, the electric bill, copy for some classified ads. The last envelope I picked up had my name on it. I thought that was a bit unusual, but didn't think much of it, until I opened it. As soon as I read what was inside, I told Toni, who immediately contacted Officer Haskins, then the sheriff's office."

"Where's the letter now?" Jim asked.

"I have it right here," Leavitt said.

"Don't touch it," Jim ordered. "I'll come around and read it."

In the center of Leavitt's desk was an index card. *The revolution has begun!* was written on it, crudely printed in blue ink.

"The revolution has begun?" Jim said aloud. "What in the blue blazes does that mean?"

"Your guess is as good as anyone's, Jim," Avery said.

"Where's the envelope?"

"It's still on my desk," Tyson answered.

Jim went over to Tyson's desk. He looked at the white number 10 sized envelope, with no return address, bearing an Austin area postmark, on it.

"Did anyone else handle this envelope, Ms. Tyson?"

"No."

"What about the card itself?"

"I handed it to Ms. Leavitt. She and I are the only ones who touched it."

"Except for who knows how many others in the postal system," Jim said. "Ms. Leavitt, Ms. Tyson, would you object to being fingerprinted?

I'd like to have your prints to compare with the ones on the envelope and note."

"Not at all," Leavitt answered.

"I have none, either," Tyson said.

"Thank you. Ms. Tyson, other than the fact you are the local reporter who has been covering these murders, can you think of any reason why this message was sent to you specifically, or who might have sent it?"

"I'm afraid I can't, Ranger."

"That's what I figured. Damn, I wish the post office still used postmarks for every town, as they did in the past. That would've narrowed down where this was sent from. Fred, soon as I obtain the ladies' fingerprints, I'm gonna take this card and envelope back to my office and run some tests on 'em. I'd bet my hat there's fingerprints on both that match the others I've collected at the crime scenes."

"I sure wouldn't take that bet."

"Neither would I, Jim," Haskins agreed. "Anything more we can do in the meantime?"

"You and Jody Kennedy just keep diggin', talking to everyone you can. Someone, somewhere, must have seen something. Except for the prints or DNA I might be able to get off the note and envelope, they won't be much help. These can be bought anywhere, from a convenience store, to a dollar store, card shop, or big box outlet."

Jim picked up the card and envelope by one

of their corners, then slid them into separate baggies.

"Be right back to take your prints, ladies."

When Jim dusted the envelope for fingerprints, two seemed to leap off the paper at him. A thumbprint, and one from an index finger, that matched those from the three murder scenes. Dusting the index card produced another match.

"That confirms the person who sent this is our killer," he muttered. "The question is, why? What's he up to? Is he just mentally ill, or is there some other reason? Whatever, he sure is one twisted individual. And he'll strike again, unless I can track him down, and fast."

He printed out all the photographs he'd taken, took more of the latest evidence, enlarged and printed those, and taped them to the walls of his office. He took the transcripts of his notes on all three killings and spread those out on his desk. He glanced at the antique Regulator clock hanging across from his desk, and sighed.

"Let's see if I can find somethin' I missed, before Lieutenant Stoker gets here."

Jim shook his head, took a gulp from his can of Dr Pepper, then began reading his notes, yet again.

Lieutenant Jameson Stoker walked into Jim's office about two hours later. He was known for his brusque, no-nonsense attitude, but often wasn't quite sure how to handle Jim, who was one of the few men in Company F who could coax a rare smile from the lieutenant.

"Howdy, Lieutenant," Jim said. "I figured you'd be comin' through my door anytime now. You want some coffee?"

"Howdy, Jim. No thanks on the coffee. I brought my own. I just can't stomach yours."

"I bought a new blend. You might like it."

"It doesn't matter what blend of coffee you buy, Ranger. No one can drink it but you."

"And Stacy Martinez. She said to tell you howdy, and that you're a big baby about coffee. I agreed with her, of course."

"You would. How're she and the baby doin'?"

"Just fine, both of 'em. Melinda's as cute as the dickens. Mike wasn't home, but Stacy said he's still floatin' on air about their new daughter."

"That's good." Stoker settled into the chair alongside Jim's desk. "You made any more progress on the Llano County killings?"

"Not much. The only new development you don't know about is the note sent to the Llano paper this morning. This is it, right here."

Jim slid the baggie holding the index card to Stoker, who read it, then removed his reading glasses.

"What the hell does that mean?"

"Pretty much anything and nothing," Jim

answered. "I'm hoping our man sends another one. That might give me more of a clue. And I'm damn sure getting impatient, waiting on the DNA results. I know the lab's backed up, but I need those. I've got good sets of prints from all the scenes, plus now on that note, but they aren't much help. Whoever this person is, he's not in any of the national or state databases. The military couldn't match up the prints, either."

"Which is why he doesn't care about leaving prints. He knows it'd be a real fluke if we found a match. As far as the lab, when I get back to Austin, I'll light another fire under 'em," Stoker promised. "What's all this you've got spread around the office?"

"Every bit of evidence I've collected," Jim answered. "I've been comparing 'em, hoping to put something together that'll help me track this maniac down, before he kills someone else. And he will."

"Sadly, I'm certain you're right, Jim. You mind if I take a look?"

"I thought you'd never ask. Stacy's seen all this, but she hasn't been able to come up with any ideas."

"How about the sheriff, or the Llano police?"

"Nothing there, either. What's really puzzling me is no one has seen any sign of the suspect, except that one sighting at the coffee shop, who may have nothing to do with this at all. So far, no luck tracking that *hombre* down, but we'll find him."

"Any information on the bastard who took those shots at you?"

"Nothing yet. I couldn't get any usable prints off the shell casings. I'm hopin' the lab will come up with some DNA traces."

"I guess we should just be grateful he hasn't tried to bushwhack you again."

"Yeah, I'm pretty happy he hasn't, that's for damn certain. Lieutenant, I'm not completely stumped. I do have a couple of theories, if you'd care to mull 'em over. I've got to confess, my first one's way out there."

"Of course I would. We both learned a long time ago some of the wackiest ideas turn out to be reality."

"Okay. Don't say I didn't warn you. Take a look at the pictures of the dead birds, which I've got tacked up on the wall. Unless, that is, you'd rather see the actual evidence. I have those birds bagged, tagged, and in the freezer right over there."

"I can do without that. I'll settle for the photos."

"I thought you would. Take a close look at the photos, and tell me what you see."

Stoker studied the photos more closely.

"All I see is three dead birds."

"That's right, three dead birds. One hung, one with a broken neck, and one crushed, each found with a victim killed in the same manner. Also, the first chicken is a Rhode Island Red. The second is a White Leghorn. It took me a bit longer to find out the duck's breed. It's a fairly rare Swedish Blue."

"You think those breeds have a special meaning for the perpetrator?"

"Not the breeds. The colors. Red, white, and blue. Could it be our suspect has some twisted sense of patriotism, and is killin' folks for the good ol' U.S. of A.?"

"You're right, Jim. That theory is so far out in space it's not even in this solar system."

"Maybe. Maybe not. Think on his victims. A lesbian, an Hispanic—unless the DNA tests come up otherwise—and a black man. Might be a neo-Nazi type we're lookin' for."

"In which case, all the more reason to find this monster, and fast," Stoker said. "If even part of what you say is true, we'll have the feds down here soon as they get wind of this. You're talking Federal hate crime charges."

"I know," Jim answered, frustration plain in his voice.

"You said you had a couple of theories. What's the other one?"

"It might be even a longer shot than my first one. Lillian Gates and her wife were growin' and sellin' marijuana. So, it turns out, was Joe Benson. Can't say about the *hombre* from Pontotoc until the lab finishes up their testing, but if he had any traces of weed on his clothes, or any in his body tissues, we could be lookin' at a fallin' out among drug dealers."

"I highly doubt that, Jim. Three brutal murders over some weed? It wouldn't be worth the trouble, or the chance of gettin' caught, knowin' the needle awaits. Now, if you were talking hard drugs, that's another story, but marijuana." Stoker hesitated and shook his head. "I doubt it."

"I know I'm graspin' at straws, Lieutenant, but drugs are the only connection I've got. That, and the fact only one of the victims was white, and she was a lesbian. If you can come up with any better thoughts, I'd certainly love to hear 'em."

"Well, Jim, let me see if I can spot something in all this."

Stoker got up to examine the photos on the wall. He'd been looking at them for ten minutes when Jim's phone rang.

"Ranger James Blawcyzk."

"Ranger Blawcyzk, Llano County Dispatch. We have another possible murder."

"Location?"

"31 Euel Moore Drive, Kingsland. That's Nguyen's Asian Wholesale Meats and Produce. Deputy Kennedy wants you to meet him at the rear of the building."

"Tell him I'm en route. ETA one hour."

"Will do, Ranger."

"Don't tell me," Stoker said, as soon as Jim hung up.

"Seems so. Over in Kingsland, this time. You want to take a ride?"

"Damn straight I do. I'm gonna take my car and follow you."

"Then let's get rollin'."

10

Luckily, the Ranch Road 2900 bridge over the Llano River, which was washed out by a major flood the previous October, had been quickly rebuilt by the Texas DOT, saving Jim a long detour. Euel Moore Drive was sealed off by Llano sheriff's department units at both ends of the block between Pioneer Lane and Loma Linda. Jim went past the roadblock at Pioneer. Nguyen's Asian Wholesale was located in a small industrial park. It was the first building on the left, surrounded by scrub-covered, empty lots.

Jim drove around to the back of the building, where Deputy Kennedy and Sheriff Avery were waiting, along with another Llano County deputy, Mark Thornton, who was attached to the Kingsland substation. The Kingsland Volunteer Fire Department rescue unit and ambulance, along with the county coroner's van, were sitting in the dirt lot behind the building.

Jim and Stoker parked their cars alongside them. As soon as they opened their doors, the overwhelming stench of decaying flesh assailed their nostrils. They walked up to the three local lawmen, who were standing behind a refrigerated box truck. Water was dripping from the rear doors. All of the men were dressed in full Hazmat suits.

"Glad you made good time, Jim," Avery said.

"Didn't have much traffic to fight," Jim answered. "This is Lieutenant Stoker, my supervisor. Lieutenant, you've already met Sheriff Avery. The deputies are Jody Kennedy and Mark Thornton. Fred, what's the situation?"

"Can't say for certain until we open this truck, but it appears to be another murder. Nguyen Tranh, the owner of this company, hasn't made any deliveries for the past three days. It's a one-man business. One of his customers, who started wondering why he couldn't reach Nguyen, came by, and found the place locked. So he called Nguyen's niece, askin' if she'd heard from her uncle, or if something was wrong. She lives way over to Beaumont, so she called my office for a welfare check. Mark can tell you the rest."

"The building was locked up tight when I got here, Ranger," Thornton said. "No lights on, no sign of anyone about the place. When I came around the back, the stink just about knocked me out. It wasn't hard to figure it was comin' from this truck. You can see there's a hose stuck under the doors. Obviously, it was left running, although it's kinked, which slowed down the volume some. There's too much water for it to be just from the cargo box defrosting. Even though they're not padlocked, I didn't open the doors.

The sheriff wanted to wait for you to arrive."

"You didn't turn off the hose?" Jim asked.

"No, sir. I didn't have a fingerprint dusting kit with me," Thornton answered.

"Jody was going to dust the faucet, Jim, but I advised him to wait until you arrived. Same for the truck," Avery said. "I thought you might prefer to do that yourself. The little bit of extra time it took you to get here won't make much of a difference, anyway. We did photograph everything, though."

"I reckon not, and havin' the pictures already taken will help," Jim said. "I'll dust the back of the truck, then the faucet. The cab can wait until later. Once I have the water shut off, we can open the cargo box, and see what we've got."

"I'll get your BDU out for you while you do that, Jim," Stoker said. "We're gonna need full protective headgear, too. If Nguyen's body is in that truck, and has been for three days, we've got a nasty biohazard situation on our hands. Sheriff, you might want to call whoever does your Hazmat cleanups, to have 'em standing by once we've finished with this truck."

"Right, Lieutenant."

"Fred, also get some tarps to block the view of this truck," Jim ordered. "I don't want anything recognizable getting on the news, so have a couple of your deputies keep those reporters and camera operators well back."

"Right, Lieutenant, Jim. Thornton, give Jack Tracy a call. Tell him we'll need a full crew out here. Then park some vehicles around this lot. Use the rescue truck and ambulance. We can drape tarps around those. If you have to, commandeer some civilian cars."

"Right away, Sheriff."

Jim had dusted the faucet, turned it off, and was now dressed in his protective clothing, standing a few feet behind the truck. Deputies Kennedy and Thornton were waiting for his permission to open the cargo box's doors.

"I want you to open those doors just far enough to let the water drain out, nice and slow. We can't have any possible evidence get washed away. If any object does happen to come out with the water, you let me or Sheriff Avery retrieve it. *Comprende?*"

Both deputies nodded.

"Go ahead. Open the doors, slow now."

Kennedy and Thornton edged the doors open, about an inch. More than a foot of water had accumulated inside the truck. The deputies were forced to press hard against the doors as it all now tried to drain out at once. It only took a few minutes for the flow to subside to barely a trickle.

"Hold it!" Jim ordered, when a decapitated chicken head floated out of the truck and onto the pavement. "Shut those doors, quick."

"What've you got there, Jim?" Stoker asked.

"A chicken's head. But it's what I see jammed up against the doors I don't want fallin' out of the truck. It's a corpse."

"What do you want my men to do, Jim?" Avery asked.

"Leave those doors open just enough so the water trickles out. Soon as it drains for a few more minutes, I'm goin' inside."

"Okay."

Kennedy and Thornton eased the doors open just far enough so the flow subsided, and held them that way until the remaining water barely dripped from the truck.

"All right," Jim said. "You can open the doors all the way. I'm goin' in."

Jim pulled his protective mask over his head, turned on his searchlight, then clambered into the truck. The first thing he saw, caught against one of the logistic tracks, was an Asian man's decapitated head. Just beyond that, caught by its ankle in a loop of cargo strap, was a bloated, headless body.

"Is that—" Avery started to question, from where he stood at the rear of the truck.

"Since I've never seen this person, I can't say," Jim answered. "I'll need you, or someone who knows him, to identify the remains. But I'd wager a month's pay we're lookin' at what's left of Nguyen Tranh, and he's been murdered. Fred, you might as well tell Maurice to get a body bag, and haul this corpse back to the morgue. After three days, locked in a cargo compartment in the hot sun, and sittin' in a foot of water besides, there's not much I can learn from it. We'll have to hope the autopsy gives us some answers."

"Okay, Jim."

"Jody, while I go through this truck, I'd like you to go through the shop. I doubt our suspect went inside, but we have to be certain."

"All right, Jim. I'll process the doors for any prints that might turn up, too."

"Good. Fred, if you'd start talking to folks who live or work around here, to see if they saw anyone suspicious, that'd be appreciated."

"I'll get right on it."

"Where can I lend a hand, Jim?" Stoker asked.

"How about you go through this truck's cab?" Jim answered. "That's the most likely place any evidence'll turn up, except for back here. Unless you'd rather deal with the media folks."

"I'll get the kit from my car and go to work on the cab," Stoker said. "I'll let you or the sheriff handle the media."

"Coward," Jim said, with a grin.

"That's right," said Stoker, with a grin of his own.

Jim went to work inside the cargo box, photographing Nguyen's head and body. When he rolled the headless corpse onto its back, he found the carcass of the decapitated chicken, which had apparently become lodged under Nguyen's remains as the water level lowered. He photographed that, then bagged it for further testing. He then removed the contents from Nguyen's pockets, bagged and labeled those.

"Guess it's time to start scrapin' for samples," Jim said to himself.

Maurice LaPointe appeared at the back of the truck, along with two Llano police officers.

"The sheriff said you're ready for me to remove the body, Ranger?" he asked.

"Yeah, Maurice. It's in even worse shape than the one from Pontotoc. Do the best you can for me, will you? Oh, and when you tag it, and write up your report, don't forget that Nguyen is the victim's last name, Tranh his first. Asians usually render their names opposite Western cultures."

"Always do my best, you know that. I do appreciate the reminder about the name, though. There's not too many Vietnamese in this part of Texas. Most of 'em are over on the Gulf, or even in Louisiana, working their shrimp boats."

LaPointe gestured to the officers to bag Nguyen's body, and take it to his waiting van. Once it was out of the truck, Jim resumed searching for evidence.

"Time to start scratchin' around for anything I

can come up with, not that I'm expectin' much," he muttered.

For the next ninety minutes, Jim combed through the cargo compartment, taking samples of anything that appeared it might reveal the slightest clue. Once he was finished, he jumped out of the truck, and removed his protective clothing. Lieutenant Stoker was waiting for him.

"You have any luck, Jim?" he asked.

"Maybe, but I doubt it," Jim answered. "How about you?"

"I found plenty of prints, but they're all the same. I'm certain they're Nguyen's. I also found a half-empty pack of cigarettes, and some butts in the ashtray. We should be able to get some good DNA results from those. It'll most likely be Nguyen's."

"Where's the sheriff, and Deputy Kennedy?"

"Avery's still talking with the neighboring business owners, and Kennedy's still inside the shop."

Stoker noticed Jim wasn't really listening, but was looking beyond him, into the distance. Jim's eyes glittered like chips of blue ice as he squinted at the thick grass across the road.

"Jim, you look like somethin's puzzling you," Stoker said.

"It is, or I guess I should say, was. I've been tryin' to figure out how the killer got in here without anyone noticing him. I think I know how he managed it."

"How?"

"He came in from the river."

"The river? What makes you think that?"

"Because it's the best way to approach this building without being seen. If the suspect drove here, or rode on a bike, someone would have noticed it in the lot. I know all the potential witnesses haven't been spoken to yet, but I'd bet my hat, if anyone had seen a vehicle in Nguyen's lot, they would have come out when they saw all the police activity, and told someone."

"It's possible someone might have noticed something, but didn't think anything of it, and went about their business, so they're no longer around here."

"Maybe, but I don't think so. My gut tells me our man came in from the river."

"I've seen too many hunches pay off to not trust your instincts, Jim."

"It's not just my instincts. If you look close, you can see where some of the brush and grass looks like it's been stepped on, and is still springing back into place. I'm gonna take a closer look. I just need to get my casting equipment out of my truck. If I'm right, with any luck there'll be some nice, clean footprints. The soil's pretty sandy, so anyone walking over it would be bound to leave tracks."

"I'm comin' with you. I'll tell one of the deputies what we're up to, so he can let the sheriff know. I'll meet you back at your truck."

When they crossed the street, Jim pointed to a barely discernable depression in the grass at its shoulder. He bent down and plucked two of the longest blades.

"See this here, Lieutenant?" He pointed to darker spots on the blades, where the stems had been broken. "This grass has been stepped on by someone, and not all that long ago. Within the past couple of days, for certain. It's startin' to dry where the blades're broken, but it's still green."

"It could have been an animal," Stoker said.

"Uh-uh." Jim shook his head. "Not likely. A small critter, like a rabbit, fox, or maybe a ground squirrel, wouldn't crush the grass like this. If it was something bigger, say a deer, the hooves would cut the grass more cleanly. Plus, look at the trail the person left. It doesn't look a'tall like an animal made it. A human walked through this scrub, sure as shootin'. Let's see where it leads us."

Jim stepped into the overgrown, waist-high grass. He turned to the left, paralleling the road.

"He went this way, Lieutenant."

"How can you tell? I can't see any difference between any of this grass and brush. It all looks the same to me."

203

Jim laughed.

"That's why y'all keep an ol' cowboy like me in the Rangers. Knowin' how to trail *muy malo hombres* has been passed down through my family for six generations. My grandpa passed it to my pa, and he passed it along to me. Soon as he's old enough, I'll pass that knowledge to Josh. I might not be a computer genius, but if you need to follow an old track through the *malpais*, then I'm the man you want.

"See, he turned a bit more into the brush here. Seems like he wanted to stay close to the road, but just far enough off it so's no one'd notice him. He's smart. He didn't come out of the water right across from Nguyen's place. Instead, he left the river a mite upstream. I reckon we'll find that spot soon as we get past this bunch of vacation cabins. Wait, here's something."

Jim plucked a small piece of teal green cloth from a low hanging branch of a small oak.

"Yup, he passed this way. Got a piece of cloth looks like it came off a T-shirt. Appears there's even a speck of blood on it. With luck, this'll place him at the scene."

He slid the cloth into a baggie.

"Let's keep movin'."

Studying the ground, Jim walked for another hundred yards, then stopped. He took off his Stetson, ran his right hand through his hair, then replaced the hat.

"Something wrong, Jim?" Stoker asked.

"I dunno. The son of a bitch just might've fooled me. I haven't seen any sign of a man passin' since a little ways after I found that cloth. Only thing I can figure is he turned back to the road. He might've parked his vehicle somewhere along here, then came back to it after he killed Nguyen."

"You think we should head back?"

Jim shook his head.

"Not yet. My gut still tells me he came in from the river. He probably didn't want to cross anyone's lawn and have someone ask what he was doin'. We'll walk a bit farther and see if I can pick up his trail again."

They walked past three more riverfront resort properties, until they came upon a short canal dug perpendicular to the Llano. On either side were half-a-dozen rectangular piers, protected by corrugated steel retaining walls. Apparently, this had been a small marina, the now badly deteriorated piers serving as docks for pleasure craft at one time, but were now abandoned, their decks and roofs gone, the dirt fill overgrown with grass and weeds. A concrete walled boat ramp that fronted directly on Euel Moore Drive was crumbling, and filled with debris. A *For Sale* sign marked the property. Jim stopped short.

"This is it, Lieutenant. Our suspect came out of

the river right here. Odds are no one'd pay any mind to him. They'd just figure he was a boater who stopped here for a bit, maybe to duck behind a bush and take a leak."

Jim hurried over to the third pier on the right. Three footprints were imprinted in the damp soil.

"Just what I was hopin' to find," Jim said, as he placed his casting kit on the ground and opened it. "Nice, clean boot prints. And unless I miss my guess, they'll match the one I found up at the llanite dike. You mind givin' me a hand makin' the casts?"

"Not at all, Jim."

After photographing the prints, mixing the dental stone and pouring it into the boot prints, Jim looked for additional evidence while he waited for the stone to dry.

"Look here, Lieutenant. This is where the *hombre* tied off his boat. You can see where the line rubbed through the dirt and moss. There's some paint from a boat on the wall, too. Our boy's startin' to get a bit sloppy. I'll take some samples. While I do that, could you call the sheriff for me? Tell him we need a boat down here, as quick as he can get us one. I want to see if I can find where this *hombre* put into the water."

"You think there's a chance you'll be able to?"

"*Quien sabe*? Probably not much of one. But I won't know unless I try."

Stoker made the call while Jim took scrapings

from the pier. He hung up just as Jim finished.

"The sheriff says he'll have a boat here in about twenty minutes. He suggested having two men ride along, one to maneuver the boat, the second to help search the riverbank. I told him I'd be that man. He's got a deputy named Claire Lamoureux who'll do the navigating."

"Can't think of anyone else I'd rather have along," Jim said. "Long as you don't get seasick."

"It's a river, Jim."

"Then, long as you don't get riversick. Not much more we can do here, except wait for the casts to dry, and scour these piers for any more evidence."

"We might want to go ask whoever owns that resort next door if they saw anyone suspicious a couple of days back," Stoker suggested. "I can do that while you poke around here."

"Good idea, Lieutenant. I'd be obliged."

"Hey, I want this bastard caught as much as you do, Jim. Because I know one thing for certain. If he isn't stopped, and soon, heads will roll."

Jim winced.

"Lieutenant, best leave the bad jokes to me. That was awful, even by my standards."

"Got ya, at long last," Stoker responded, with a deep laugh.

One of the groundskeepers at the resort neighboring the abandoned marina had, in fact, seen a boater arrive at the abandoned marina, but wasn't clear on the man's description. He was certain the man didn't have long hair, and wore a dark blue or black baseball cap. When Lieutenant Stoker suggested the person he saw might have tucked his hair up under the cap, the groundskeeper admitted that was a possibility, but didn't believe he had. He had waved to the groundskeeper, then walked up the road, in the direction of Nguyen's warehouse. After that brief encounter, the groundskeeper had returned to his work. He hadn't noticed when the man returned. Frustrated at another dead end, all Jim could do was take to the river, knowing finding any sign of where his quarry had left the water was a long shot, at best.

After cruising the riverbanks in both directions for over an hour, Jim finally had to admit there was no possible way of finding the spot where his quarry had left the river. They were just pulling back into the abandoned marina when Jim's phone rang.

"Jim, it's Fred. Where are you right now?"

"Back where we started from. We're just about to get out of the river. Why? Did you find something?"

"No, but my office received a call from *The Llano News*. They apparently got another note in today's mail. How soon can you get back there?"

"That depends. I've probably got another hour

or so here to finish up. Then it's twenty minutes or so to Llano. If we don't get back before the office closes, will someone wait for us?"

"Let me check. I'll call you right back."

"All right."

"What've you got, Jim?" Stoker asked.

"The Llano newspaper got another message from our killer. The sheriff's calling to make certain they'll wait for us to get back there. He's callin' right back."

"Ranger Blawcyzk, I can save you some time by leavin' the boat tied up here for now," Deputy Lamoureux suggested. "I'll drive you and the lieutenant back to Nguyen's warehouse, then return for the boat."

"That's an excellent idea, Deputy," Jim agreed. "We'd be obliged."

"No problem at all."

Jim's phone rang.

"Yeah, Fred?"

"This message was also sent to Bonnie Tyson. She and Ms. Leavitt will wait as long as necessary."

"*Bueno*. We'll see you in a few minutes."

Using her lights, but no siren, Deputy Lamoureux set a quick pace on the return trip.

"Hold on a minute, Deputy," Jim ordered, when they approached the roadblock at Pioneer Lane. "Pull over and stop here for a minute."

"You see something, Jim?" Stoker asked.

"I sure do. You see that black Rolls-Royce pulled into the dirt lot up ahead?"

"I sure do."

"That's the Hannaford-Smythes' car. The folks who found the body in Pontotoc. I'm beginning to wonder if they're telling the truth, or runnin' a windy on me?"

"You mean like they had something to do with the man's death?"

"Or at least put the body there."

"But why would they report finding the body, if they had something to do with the man's murder?" Lamoureux asked.

"If I could answer that question, I'd buy a lottery ticket," Jim answered. "But it gets even more interesting. See that yellow Accord parked next to the Rolls?"

"The one with the couple sitting on the hood?"

"That's the one. The car is Clarence Sloan's. The couple is him and his on-again, off-again girlfriend, Laura Webb. The woman who will soon be sole owner of Joe Benson's coffee shop."

"I'd say that's quite the coincidence," Stoker said.

"I'd say what the hell are they doin' here, all of 'em? Conveniently parked alongside each other," Lamoureux added.

"Bingo, both of you. Why would they be here, rather'n back in Llano, particularly the English folks, who should have left town by now. Deputy, they all know me, and Deputy Kennedy," Jim said. "Probably Investigator Haskins from the Llano P.D., too. I don't want to spook any of 'em by asking them more questions, at least not right now. Would you mind keepin' an eye on 'em for a few days, and let me know if they do anything suspicious? I'll clear it with the sheriff."

"I sure would, Ranger. That'll give me a break from pullin' over speeders and drunk drivers."

"*Bueno*. I'm obliged. "Let's get goin', before they notice us."

"Sure thing."

Ninety minutes later, Jim, Lieutenant Stoker, and Sheriff Avery were back at the *Llano News* office. Several television satellite units were parked in the lot across the street, in front of the courthouse square.

"Howdy, ladies," Jim said, when he walked into the office. "We're sorry to keep you waiting, but we had to complete our investigation in Kingsland."

"We understand," Toni Leavitt said. "The message is still on Bonnie's desk."

The envelope which evidently contained the latest missive was lying on Tyson's desk, still unopened.

"You haven't opened it, Ms. Tyson?" Jim asked.

"No, Ranger. Once I saw it was addressed to

me, and had no return address, I just knew it had to be from the same person who sent the last one."

"Excellent. I'll give it a quick dusting for fingerprints, then open 'er up and see what we've got."

After dusting the envelope, and obtaining several clear prints, Jim slit it open. A single index card slipped out. A cryptic message was written on it, in the same crude printing and blue ink as the first. Jim read the message aloud.

"The killings will stop when the killings stop."

"Exactly what the hell is that supposed to mean?" Avery exclaimed.

"Not much," Jim said. "Off the top of my head, either this *hombre* is sayin' the killings will stop when he's ready for them to, or he's talking about some other killings entirely, that he's upset about. If so, that means these are revenge murders. It sure isn't much help."

"He's not trying to keep his actions a secret," Stoker said. "He's sending notes, he's left plenty of prints, and once we get the DNA results, we'll know quite a bit more about whomever he is."

"He's got to realize his fingerprints aren't on record anywhere," Jim said. "That means he's not ex-military or law enforcement, doesn't have a job where fingerprinting is a requirement to be hired, and has no arrest record. But so far, he's been danged good at coverin' his tracks. Until

I can figure out a pattern, he's gonna be hard to catch. Ms. Leavitt, I'm going to have a Llano police officer guard you and your staff, at least until I'm certain one of you won't be his next target. Ms. Tyson, I'd like you to accept 'round the clock protection, since for some reason our suspect seems fixated on you."

"Are you certain that's necessary, Ranger?" Leavitt asked.

"Even if he isn't, I am," Avery answered.

"I would feel safer," Tyson said.

"Good. Then that's settled," Jim said.

"What's your next step, Jim?" Stoker asked.

"Right now, waitin' for the damn lab to get those DNA results to me. That, and keep on tryin' to figure out who this *hombre* is, and his motive. Ms. Leavitt, I have to ask you if you, or any of your staff, have seen anyone you don't know hanging around your office? Particularly a white male with long, dark hair?"

"No, Ranger, we haven't."

Jim looked at the office's walls, which were covered with old advertisements for services offered by a long-ago barber shop.

"This building's pretty old," he said. "Looks like it was home to a tonsorial parlor back some time ago."

"Do you mean a barber shop?" Tyson asked.

"Yes. In the eighteen-hundreds, that's what a barber shop was called. It usually offered shaves and baths along with haircuts. Quite a few barbers also provided crude medical procedures, such as bleeding. Their age is the reason I'm interested in these walls. There's a good possibility someone could have found, or made himself, a peephole from either of the adjoining buildings."

"That's highly unlikely," Leavitt said. "On one side is the courthouse annex, which is a much newer building. On the other is an attorney's office. It would be virtually impossible for someone to spy on us without being discovered."

"I agree with you, Ms. Leavitt; however, I'd still like to search the neighboring offices," Jim answered. "That doesn't have to be done tonight, though. It's already late, well past sun-down. I'll have Deputy Kennedy do that, at your con-venience. Since today's Friday, that can wait until Monday. It's time for everyone, myself included, to take a step back for a day or so. A pause to gather my thoughts might lead me to something I've overlooked. Ladies, I thank you for waiting. I'm obliged. Good night."

"Good night, Ranger."

"Jim, there's a whole passel of media folks outside," Stoker said. "They must've followed us from Kingsland. One of us is gonna have to make a statement."

"I'll take care of it, Lieutenant. Fred, I guess you'll have to stick around a few more minutes, to make certain none of these reporters bother Ms. Leavitt or Ms. Tyson when they leave."

"That won't be a problem."

"*Gracias*. C'mon, Lieutenant, let's go face those people."

As soon as Jim and the lieutenant came out of the newspaper's office, strobe lights came on, television cameras were lifted to shoulders, and microphones were shoved in Jim's and Stoker's faces.

"Just back off a minute," Jim ordered. "I'm going to make a statement about today's developments. I will say nothing beyond that. There will be no questions taken afterwards."

Jim waited for the reporters to get in position before he started.

"As most of you know, I am Texas Ranger James Blawcyzk, of Company F in Waco. I am covering Llano County while the Ranger normally assigned to it is on maternity leave. With me today is Lieutenant Jameson Stoker, again of Company F. As you also know, the Rangers, along with the Llano County Sheriff's Department, have been investigating several recent murders. The latest of those took place today in Kingsland. I cannot divulge any further information about that particular killing, including the victim's identity, until the next of kin are notified."

"The reason we are here at *The Llano News*

215

office is the paper has received two messages, ostensibly from the suspect. I cannot confirm that at this time, nor reveal their contents.

"At this point, all indications are the crimes have been committed by the same person. We have found no connection between any of the victims; however, we also have reason to believe these are not random attacks. Today's victim, as were the previous three, was found with a dead fowl. Until now, we have not revealed that the fowl found with each victim was killed in the same manner. We have been unable to determine a motive, nor the reason the suspect is killing chickens or ducks and leaving their carcasses with the victims' bodies.

"We do have several good leads, including fingerprints. We are awaiting results of DNA testing, which should narrow our search. We also have one fairly credible eyewitness description of a possible suspect, a white male, thin, with long hair and a beard. At the time he was seen, he was wearing a T-shirt, dark pants, and a baseball cap. He may be riding a green bicycle.

"While we have no reason to believe the general public is in any danger, naturally, everyone should take the usual precautions for their safety. Make certain all doors, windows, and vehicles are locked. Be aware of your sur-roundings. If you see anyone suspicious, do not approach the person, but call your local police department, sheriff's office, or the Texas Rangers immediately. The person we are looking for should be considered armed, and extremely dangerous. He has already killed four people, and would no doubt have no compunction about killing again. That is all I have to say at this time. Any further information or statements will come from Company F Headquarters. Thank you."

Ignoring the reporters' shouts, Jim and Stoker went to their vehicles.

"Don't forget, we've got the team penning on Sunday, Lieutenant," Jim said, as he opened the Tahoe's door. "You're still gonna show up, aren't you?"

"Yeah, I'll be there." Stoker shook his head. "How you ever talked me into ridin' a horse and chasin' cows around, I'll never know."

"Because it's for a good cause, and you know it."

"I reckon you're right. The Blanco County Women Veteran's Aid Association certainly needs more funds."

"That's the only reason I'm takin' part. Hell, with you and Bruce as my partners we don't have a chance of comin' anywhere near winning time. But we'll have fun. You headed back to San Antonio tonight?"

"No, I've got to swing by my sister's in Austin, so I'm staying with her for the weekend. My wife's gone to visit family in Baton Rouge, so there's no point in me goin' home, anyway. I'll see you at the rodeo grounds."

"See you Sunday."

Jim and Stoker left Llano via Texas 71, a two-lane highway which was the most direct route to Austin. The road headed southeast through mostly rolling terrain, mainly farm and ranchlands. They had gone about fifteen miles, with the lieutenant about a quarter-mile before Jim. As they approached Honey Creek, without warning, Stoker's white Dodge Charger swerved to the right. It left the road, climbed an embankment, and continued its entire length before plunging into the shallow creek, sunk to the frame in the sandy bottom. Steam rose from the smashed radiator.

"What the hell?" Jim exclaimed, when he saw Stoker's vehicle leave the road. He flipped on his strobe lights, gunned the Tahoe, and grabbed the mic for his radio.

"Ranger Unit 810 to Dispatch."

"Ranger 810, go ahead."

"Serious MVA on Texas 71 East, at the Honey Creek overpass. Single Texas Ranger vehicle involved. Vehicle is in creek. Unknown injuries. Send EMS and state troopers. On scene now."

"10-4, Ranger 810. Will send assistance. Dispatch, out."

"Ranger 810, out."

Jim pulled his truck to the side of the road, jumped the guard rail, and scrambled into the creek. Stoker was still inside his vehicle, attempting to open the jammed driver's door.

"Get out the other side!" Jim yelled. He ran around the back of the Dodge and tugged on the front passenger door. It resisted his efforts, but opened just enough for Stoker to slide across the seat and squeeze out.

"You all right, Lieutenant?" Jim asked.

"Yeah. Yeah, I think so," Stoker replied.

"I've got an ambulance on the way, just in case. What happened? You fall asleep?"

Stoker gave Jim a withering look.

"Damn you, Jim, you know me better than that. No, I didn't fall asleep. Some damn son of a bitch shot me off the road. Just missed me."

"What?"

"You heard me. Someone tried to kill me, and damn near succeeded. Windshield shattered when the bullet hit it. Piece of glass must've cut my neck."

"Lemme see."

Jim took a closer look at the bloody slash along the right side of Stoker's neck.

"I don't think glass did this, Lieutenant. That slug came closer than you realized." He glanced at Stoker's wrecked car.

"The back window's not busted. That means the

slug is most likely still in your car somewhere. Soon as it's pulled outta this creek, I'll search it. Let's get up on the bank while we wait for help."

"Sure. I wasn't ready for a bath, yet, anyway."

Several motorists had stopped. Two of them were descending the riverbank to offer assistance. Stoker waved them off.

"I can climb this bank without any help," he muttered.

"You still need to be checked out," Jim said. "That was quite a wreck. I know this is a long shot, but did you happen to see where that shot came from?"

"You won't believe this, but I think I did. There's a pull out for an historical marker on the other side of the road, just past the creek. I thought I saw a rifle flash from there. Of course, it might just have been a reflection from my headlights."

"You're not buyin' that any more'n I am. Soon as the troopers get here, I'll go take a look."

They had reached the top of the bank, where the passersby had gathered in a group.

"You fellers all right?" one of them asked.

"Yeah, I am," Stoker answered.

"What happened, Ranger? You get run off the road or somethin'?"

"Yeah. Or somethin'."

"I've got an ambulance on the way for him," Jim said. "Any of you folks happen to see a vehicle parked by the historical marker? One that might've pulled away real fast, probably with its lights off?"

One woman spoke up.

"I might've seen one, yeah. About a half-mile back, a car headin' east blew by me probably doin' better'n a hundred or so. Damn fool only had his parking lights on."

"Thanks, ma'am," Jim answered. "I don't suppose you noticed what type of vehicle it was?"

"Just that it was a light-colored car, not a pickup or SUV. It was goin' way too fast for me to catch much else."

"Even that'll help. Lieutenant, he's probably long gone, but I'm gonna have roadblocks set up at County 307 and another at U.S. 281. Maybe we'll get lucky."

"He could turn off anywhere along this road," Stoker said.

"I know. I'm just hopin' he doesn't."

"Is there anything we can do, Ranger?" another passerby asked.

"A couple of things," Jim answered. "Unfortunately, you'll all have to stay here until you can be questioned. It won't take all that long. Also, if you would stay with Lieutenant Stoker, here, until the EMTs arrive, I'll go take a look around that pull out right now."

"Be happy to."

"*Bueno*. I'll be back quick as I can."

Jim got in his truck and drove to the pull out, parking on the side of the highway so as not to disturb any possible evidence. He took out his evidence kit and flashlight. He shone the light on a set of tire tracks, as well as several footprints. He stopped and whistled when his light's beam caught a glint of metal, just behind two boulders set near the marker. He took out his tweezers and picked up an empty shell casing.

"Same caliber as the one that nicked me," he muttered. "Guaranteed, once we do the ballistics, they'll show it came from the same gun. Those boot prints look mighty damn familiar, too. Bet they match the one I found at the cemetery. Those marks on top of the rock look like the same ones as at Baby Head, too."

A Highway Patrol Suburban pulled up behind Jim's Tahoe.

"You the Ranger in the accident?" the trooper called.

"No, he's on the other side of the bridge," Jim answered. "And it wasn't an accident. This is now a crime scene. I need you to stay with my lieutenant while I process some evidence here. I'll be with you soon as I'm done."

"You've got it."

The trooper drove on. Jim got his casting kit. After taking photos of the boulders, tire and boot prints, he mixed some dental stone to begin taking their impressions.

• • •

It was over an hour before the tow truck arrived, and Stoker's car was winched out of the creek. The driver had already been instructed not to load the vehicle until it could be examined. The passersby had all been interviewed, most of them having gone on their way. Stoker's neck wound had been treated, the EMTs then returning to Llano.

"If the bullet's still in here, it won't take me long to find it, Lieutenant," Jim said. He opened the Dodge's left rear door and shone his flashlight on the back seat. A ragged hole, halfway up the backrest, was evident.

"I've got it already. Just have to dig it out."

Jim took out his jackknife and widened the bullet hole, then took a pair of forceps and shoved them into the seat.

"Got it!" he exclaimed, when the forceps hit a hard object. He grasped that with them, and pulled it out.

"Here's our bullet," he said, holding it up. "If this doesn't match the one that clipped me, I'll eat 'em both, without any salt, pepper, or even ketchup."

"You need anythin' else out of this car?" the tow truck operator asked.

"Not right now," Jim answered. "It will need to go to the D.P.S. garage in Austin. You can follow us there. Lieutenant, you can ride with me. I'll drop you at your sister's on my way home."

"All right. You might not have to take me as far as my sister's, though. There should be a car I can get from the D.P.S. garage."

Once the lieutenant's wrecked car was loaded on the flatbed, they continued the drive to Austin.

"You're gonna be sore for a few days, Lieutenant," Jim said. "You got bounced around pretty good."

"I know. That's not what's on my mind, Jim. What *is* on my mind is who took that shot at me. Assuming it's our suspect, that means he knows most of our moves almost before we do."

"My question is, why the hell is he tryin' to kill a Ranger?" Jim said. "Is it to kill whoever's investigating the murders? Or are the murders to lure whomever it is, meaning me, and now you, into a trap?"

"I dunno." Stoker shook his head. "You would think he'd have gone after one of the local law officers first. Also, he wouldn't have had any idea I'd be with you today. It was purely a coincidence."

"One which nearly got you killed. Other funny thing is, why didn't he try for me tonight? I would've been an easy target, once I got out of my truck."

"Too many questions, and not enough answers. You mind if I get some shut-eye while you drive?"

"Not at all. Maybe I'll grab a few winks too."

"So you can finish that bastard's work for him? Not a good idea, Ranger."

Jim laughed.

"I know. You think you'll still be able to make the team penning on Sunday?"

"After tonight? You're damn certain I will. This ain't gonna stop me."

11

Sunday morning, Jim and his family were at the Blanco County Fair and Rodeo Grounds, outside of Johnson City, for the Sixth Annual Texas Rangers and Texas State Troopers Charity Team Penning. Jim had unloaded Copper, as well as two horses he had borrowed from a rancher friend, and had them tied to his four-horse trailer, which was attached to a new Silverado crew cab pickup he'd recently purchased. The horses were munching on the contents of their hay nets, while Jim and his mother brushed them. Josh was napping in his portable playpen, with Kim keeping a close watch over him.

"Where the devil are Bruce and the lieutenant?" Jim grumbled, as he gave Copper another swipe of the curry comb. "They both should've been here by now. The penning's gonna start in less than an hour. If we draw one of the first slots, and they're not here, we'll be disqualified."

"Jim, for a lawman, you sure can be a worrier," Betty said. "They'll be here."

"They'd better be. We need to get these horses into the warm-up ring before we take 'em into the arena. We've got to work some of the vinegar out of 'em."

"You can stop worrying, Jim," Kim said. "Isn't that Bruce's car coming up now?"

She pointed to a white Ford Expedition as it slowly approached.

"Yeah, it is. That looks like Lieutenant Stoker's pickup bchind him, too. About time."

Jim flagged down the cars. They pulled up alongside Jim's rig and stopped. Once Texas Ranger Bruce Sherman, who was assigned to Company B and worked out of McKinney, and Lieutenant Stoker were out of their vehicles, Jim shouted at them.

"What in the world took you two knuckleheads so long? Another twenty minutes and we just might've had to go into the arena cold. Bad enough I'm the only one who's ever done this before, but tryin' to pen on cold horses is dang nigh impossible."

"Take it easy, Jim," Stoker said. "We're both here, aren't we? I'll admit I took a wrong turn, but got back on track just as Bruce was comin' down the road. No need to get all bent out of shape. And who are you callin' a knucklehead?"

"You, Lieutenant. You and Bruce both. We're not on duty."

"Ah, but sooner or later, we will be again. You might want to keep that in mind, Ranger."

"All I want to do is win this thing, for once. I'm tired of the Rangers from out in west Texas, or up in the panhandle, sayin' us men from this part of the state can't work cows, just because there ain't as many brushland ranches here, compared to their territories."

"Then you might have wanted to find better teammates than us," Bruce answered, laughing. "Although I did watch a penning on R.F.D. TV last night."

"So did I," Stoker said. "So we're all ready. Just point us in the right direction."

"Hardly. It's the direction you two yahoos are pointed in *after* we get in there that has me worried. And if I could have found other partners, I would've. Everyone else was already partnered up."

"Are you three boys going to stop fighting, and say howdy to everyone else, Jameson?" Lana, Stoker's wife, asked.

"I reckon."

Bruce's wife Kelle, and his two sons, Wyatt and Marshall, were with him. Stoker's daughter Alysha, along with his wife, accompanied him. Everyone had just finished exchanging greetings when Jim spotted another familiar vehicle entering the rodeo grounds.

"Lieutenant, you're not gonna believe this," he said. "Take a look at the car that just rolled in."

"The English folks!" Stoker exclaimed. "You can't hardly miss that Rolls. I thought they'd have headed for parts unknown by now."

"Every time I see them, I wonder more'n more what they're really up to," Jim said. "But I'm not gonna worry about 'em now. The only thing on my mind today is winning this competition."

"Jim, when you called and asked me to ride, you said it was just for fun, and a good cause," Bruce objected.

"That was until Todd Lillis and Travis Benton of Company E showed up again this year. They've been taunting me for the last three events that Paints can't win at penning, only quarter horses. This year, we're gonna win, and the two of you are gonna make certain we do. Bet all of our hats on it."

"You really think we can pull it off, with the two of us hardly ever having been in a saddle, let alone chase cows?" Stoker asked.

"And with no practice?" Bruce added.

"Jody loaned me two of his best cow ponies," Jim answered. "You just listen to me, then let the horses do the work. They've got plenty of cow savvy, so if you allow 'em to do their job, we'll do just fine. So let's get the horses saddled and get to work. Lieutenant, you'll ride Sparky. He's the buckskin overo. Bruce, Fritz is your mount. He's the bay tobiano."

"The which?"

"The dark brown and white one. The saddles and bridles are in the tack compartment. They've all got nameplates with the horses' names on 'em.

I'm certain you both must know which end of the saddle is which."

"However, how about which end of the *horse* is which?" Kelle asked. She laughed.

"Thanks for the vote of confidence, sweetheart," Bruce answered.

"All I'm asking is you don't get hurt," Kelle answered.

"All *I'm* asking is he stays on his horse, and doesn't get dumped," Jim said. "That goes for you too, Lieutenant. C'mon, I'll introduce you to your horses."

The National Anthem had just played, and the announcer was narrating his opening announcement.

"Ladies and Gentlemen, welcome to the Sixth Annual Texas Rangers and Texas State Troopers Charity Team Penning. All proceeds from this event go to the Blanco County Women Veteran's Aid Association. We thank you for your support and generosity."

"For those of you who have not attended a team penning previously, I'll give a brief description of the rules. There are three men or women on a team. In the arena is a herd of thirty yearling cows. The cows are wearing numbered collars, from zero through nine, three cows with each number. They will be held at one end of the arena. At the opposite end is a pen.

A random number will be called. At that point, a team will have sixty seconds to cut the three cows wearing that number from the herd, drive them down and into the pen. No 'trash' cows, that is, cows wearing any number but the one called, are allowed to cross the foul line, or the team will receive 'no time' for that go-round. Each team will have three go-rounds. The team with the fastest accumulated time for those will win the competition. We have a total of sixteen teams today, so get ready for some fast-moving action."

"Quiet. They're about to call out the running order," Jim said.

"Our first team is team thirteen: Texas Rangers James Blawcyzk and Lieutenant Jameson Stoker of Company F, and Ranger Bruce Sherman of Company B. Second team will be team eight: Texas Rangers Todd Lillis, Travis Benton, and John Drew of Company E. Third will be team ten: State Troopers Miguel Vazquez, Dalton Hobbs, and Reno McGarvey of Region Three. Team thirteen, please enter the arena, team thirteen. Team eight, on deck."

"Damn. I was hopin' we'd be down further in the order, when the cows are a little tired, and we'd had more time to warm up our horses," Jim said. "Well, let's mount up."

"Good luck, Jim," Kim called, as he pulled himself into the saddle.

"Yeah, right," Jim muttered under his breath, while he waved at her.

"Ride 'em, cowboy," Kelle yelled to Bruce, who wore a doubtful expression on his face.

"I'll do my best," he replied.

"Remember the plan," Jim said to Stoker and Bruce, as they rode up to the gate. "I'll cut out the first cow, and chase it down to the pen, while you two keep any others, especially trash, from breakin' away and gettin' over the foul line. Soon as I've got mine penned, you go after the next one, Lieutenant, then Bruce'll go after the third."

"Hell, those ain't cows," Stoker said. "Those are steers."

"What the hell kind of Texan are you, Lieutenant?" Jim said. "All cattle in a herd are called cows, been that way since the earliest cattle drives. Don't matter whether they're boys or gals, they're all cows."

"Bet it matters to them," Bruce said, chuckling.

"I'm a city Texan, from San Antonio," Stoker said. "The only things I know about cows are they give me cream for my coffee and are mighty tasty on a plate."

Jim sighed.

"It's gonna be a long day. A real long day."

Todd Lillis and his partners were waiting near the in gate when Jim's team rode up.

"Hey, Blawcyzk, I see you've got two new partners . . . again," Lillis taunted. "Ain't you ever gonna learn you don't stand a chance? Not with that spotted crowbait. And dang, Jim, your new teammates don't seem like they've spent much time in the saddle, not at all. Pardon my sayin' so, Lieutenant."

"We'll do just fine, Lillis," Jim shot back. "Just try'n stay in your saddle. It's plumb embarrassing when a Ranger can't even ride his own hoss."

"You care to make a little wager on that, Blawcyzk?" Benton challenged.

"Wagering's illegal in Texas."

"You just don't want to give up any of your money," Drew retorted.

"Jim, I believe we can make an exception, just this once," Stoker said. "You boys are on. A hundred dollars apiece says we whip your sorry butts."

"A hundred bucks? You're on, Lieutenant," Drew answered. "Even though I think you're plumb *loco*. No offense."

"None taken. Just hope you don't take offense when you're handin' over the cash. You in, Bruce?"

"You betcha."

"Jim?"

"I dunno." Jim shook his head. "I have to agree with John. It's a plumb *loco* bet."

"You admittin' you're gonna lose to us . . . yet again, Blawcyzk?" Lillis said.

"Hold on just a minute. I never said that. I'm

in, *if* you up the ante to two hundred between me'n you, Lillis."

"You serious?"

"Damn straight I'm serious."

"Then, it's a bet. This'll be the easiest two hundred I've ever made."

"Don't start puttin' those bills in your wallet before they're in your hand. C'mon, Lieutenant, Bruce. Let's show these dime store cowboys how it's done. Open the gate, pardner."

" 'Bout time, Ranger. I figured you'd never stop your wranglin' and actually get into the arena," the gate man said. "Here ya go."

He swung the gate open to let Jim and his teammates ride in. They went to the far end of the arena and waited for the number to be called.

"Zero. Your number is zero."

"Let's go get one, Copper," he said, putting his horse into a trot.

The crowd, the announcer's voice as he described the action, even his competitors disappeared from Jim's thoughts, as he concentrated on the herd, looking for one of the cows wearing that number. His gaze settled on a brindle cow in the middle of the herd, up against the fence.

"That one, Copper. It's in the toughest spot to cut out. We'll take it and leave the easier ones for Bruce and Stoker."

Jim nudged Copper's sides with his boot heels, urging him into the midst of the cows. Copper was a well-trained cow pony, and his instincts kicked in. He knew which cow his rider wanted, and he walked straight into the herd, singling out the brindle. He shoved the cow along the fence, keeping it between that and the other cows, so it didn't have much room to turn back. Once they cleared the herd, Jim put Copper into a gallop, which forced the cow into a run. When it made a sharp left turn, trying to return to its companions, Copper reacted instantly, cutting it off and driving it back toward the pen. He pushed the cow even harder. Stoker had left Bruce to watch the herd, while he blocked the cow's escape route on the opposite side of the arena. Jim drove the cow into the pen, then spun Copper around.

"Lieutenant, behind you! Stop that white trash cow before it crosses the foul line!"

Stoker turned his horse, but not fast enough. Seeing the cow was going to cross the line before Stoker could stop it, Jim whirled Copper, dug his heels into the big paint's ribs, and cut diagonally across the arena, turning the white cow just before it crossed the line.

"Go get your cow, Lieutenant!" he shouted. "That bald-faced one on the right side. He's at the edge, so he should be easy to cut out. Bruce, you keep the rest of those cow critters bunched. We don't want 'em to stampede for the other end. I'll turn back any that do try."

Stoker moved slowly but deliberately, cutting out his cow, which seemed docile enough, and moving it at a walk toward the pen.

"A little faster, Lieutenant, *please,*" Jim muttered, agonizing as the seconds ticked off. "No!"

Just when Stoker had the cow at the pen's gate, it broke away, luckily straight at Jim. Copper reacted without being asked, and turned the cow back in Stoker's direction. Stoker shoved it into the pen.

"Get yours, Bruce," Jim shouted. "And be quick about it. Time's runnin' out."

Bruce weaved his horse back and forth through the herd, seeking the last zero cow. When he reached it, it tried to duck between two others.

"Let your horse work him, Bruce!" Jim called. Bruce nodded, and loosened his reins a bit. Given his head, Fritz countered the cow's every zig and zag, until it was out of the herd. The horse then kept the cow moving at a fast trot. When they reached the pen, Jim and Copper helped get the cow through the gate. Jim raised his right hand for time.

"That was some nice work by Ranger Jim Blawcyzk and his horse Copper," the announcer said. "Stopped that trash cow in the nick of time."

There was a moment of quiet while everyone waited for the time.

"Team thirteen, your time is fifty-eight point eight seconds," the announcer called, a moment later. "Fifty-eight point eight. Team four, please enter the arena. Team ten, on deck."

"Blawcyzk, you and your partners want to just hand over our money now?" Todd Lillis asked, as they passed each other. "You're makin' this just too easy."

"Not on your life, Lillis," Jim retorted. "There's two more go-rounds. We just started a little slow, that's all."

"Yeah, right." Lillis threw back his head and laughed.

"Sorry, Jim," Stoker said, "I guess I should've moved a bit faster."

"Don't worry about it, Lieutenant. Better to be slow and deliberate than too fast, and lose your cow. At least we didn't come up with a no time. We're still in this thing."

"Sure was harder than it looked on the videos I watched," Bruce said. "Those cows have minds of their own."

"That's for certain," Jim said.

"Jim, a white trash cow?" Stoker said, shaking his head. "I've heard of white trash people, and white trash trailer park folks, but never of white trash cows."

"It was white, and it wasn't one of ours," Jim answered. "That makes it a white trash cow."

They'd arrived back at Jim's rig.

"Jim, you looked great out there," Kelle said.

"What about me?" Bruce asked.

"You looked like a man who hasn't been on a horse all that much, I have to say."

"Me'n Wyatt thought you did real good, Dad," Marshall piped up.

"For his first time, he did," Jim answered. "Your father did too, Alysha."

"At least none of you fell off," Lana said.

"I'm sorry I didn't get to see your ride, but Josh is still sleeping," Kim said. "I'll catch your next one."

"That's okay, honey. Bruce, Lieutenant, let's get these horses tied, the bridles off and their cinches loosened, so they can cool off. I've got some Rounders treats for them. We'll see if they want a drink, too. Then we'll watch the next few go-rounds."

While they were caring for the horses, the time for team four came over the P.A.

"Team four, your time is nineteen point two seconds. Nineteen point two."

Jim shook his head.

"Damn."

"Was that a fast time?" Bruce asked.

"It sure was. Hardly ever seen one faster."

"So we're out a bunch of cash," Stoker said.

"Not by a long shot. There's still two more go-rounds. I'll try and think up a new strategy."

Jim and his partners were the eighth team to go in the second go-round.

"You both remember how we're gonna do it this time, right?" Jim asked, as they waited outside the gate for the previous team to exit the arena.

"Yeah," Bruce said. "You'll be the cutter, and'll separate all the cows from the herd. Then you'll pass them off to me, and I'll get 'em down to the pen."

"And I'll turn back any trash cow that tries to run outta the herd, and help Bruce get his cow into the pen, if need be."

"That's right," Jim answered. "Let's get in there, and git'r done."

"Nice run," he said to the previous team, as they exited. "Keeps you in the running."

"Thanks, Jim," Trooper Pete Hawkins, team sixteen's leader, answered. "Good luck to you fellers."

"We need all of it we can get," Bruce said.

"I wasn't gonna go there, but since you brought it up, yep, you sure do."

Hawkins shook his head and chuckled.

Once Jim's team was in place, the announcer called out their cows' number.

"Number three. Your number is three."

"There's one right in front," Jim said. "You two get ready."

Jim cut the cow out of the herd, pushed it toward the pen and passed it along to Bruce. Several others started to follow it. Stoker, whooping and hollering, sent Sparky straight at them, turning them back. At the same time, Jim sent Copper into the middle of the herd, cut out the second number three cow, and drove it along the fence until Bruce picked it up. Bruce was little more than halfway to the pen when Jim spotted the third number three, hiding behind a larger, bald-faced red cow.

"Lieutenant, keep that red cow from comin' after me!" he yelled. Jim cut his target cow out from behind the red one. When he began to push his toward the pen, the red one tried to follow. Stoker put himself between Copper and the cow, driving it back toward the herd.

Jim and Bruce teamed up, one on each side of the cow, as they chased it into the pen. Jim raised his hand for time. They waited anxiously for the result.

"Team thirteen, your time is thirty seconds flat. Thirty seconds. Team one, please enter the arena. Team nine, on deck."

"Yes! That's more like it," Jim said. He leaned over and patted Copper's neck. "Good job, pard."

"You boys did great," Kim said, once they exited the arena. "It was marvelous the way you worked."

"It was pretty good, wasn't it?" Jim said, grinning.

"I'd say it was damn fine," Stoker added.

"Jameson, I never realized you could ride a horse," Lana said.

"I can't, at least, not very well. But I made a bet with Jim. If we win today, I don't have to listen to his jokes for a month."

"If that's not incentive, I don't know what is," Bruce said.

"I sure don't recollect makin' that bet, Lieutenant," Jim said. "Right now, let's take care of these horses. There's only two more teams in the first half of this go-round before the lunch break. The cows'll be changed out during the break, too. That means a fresh herd for our last run. They'll most likely be pretty rank."

"As rank as you three are starting to smell?" Kelle asked.

"I doubt that's possible," Lana said.

"Wait'll the end of the day," Jim said. "Now, I'm starved. Soon as we get the horses settled, we'll hit the food stand."

Jim's team was the fourth to last one to go in the third go-round.

"Bruce, Lieutenant, listen close," he said, as they rode toward the arena. "The teams after us are too far down to pass us, no matter how good their last runs are. That's the good news. The bad news is we're still in sixth place. The worse news is Lillis and his team still have a solid hold on first place. I ain't gonna let them win again this year. We *have* to come in under seventeen seconds."

"Jim, I don't know much about penning, but that seems awful tough," Bruce said.

"It's not awful tough. It's damn near impossible. That's why I'm gonna take a huge gamble. I'm gonna cut all three cows out, and push 'em down to the pen. I'll get 'em separated from the others and run 'em to the foul line. Once I have the last one, I'll drive all three into the pen. You fellas will have two jobs. One, keep the cows I've cut out from gettin' past us and back to the herd. Two, make certain no trash gets anywhere near the foul line. Think you can do it?"

"We'll do our best, Jim," Stoker said.

"That's good enough for me. Let's git'r done."

The three men bumped fists, then rode into the arena. Jim nodded to the judges once they were set.

"Number four. Your number is four."

Jim didn't hesitate. He put Copper into a long-reaching lope, scanning the herd as he approached. Two of the number four cows were in the far back of the herd, with a trash cow in between.

"Hyahh. Let's get 'em, Copper!"

Jim pushed his big paint through the middle of the bunched cows. He cut out the two number fours, along with the third cow with them.

"Hup! Hup!"

Jim cut all three animals from the herd. As soon as they were clear, he put Copper between the cow on the left and the trash cow. He got in front of the trash, stopped Copper, and spun him on his back heels, facing down the trash while the other two cows ran past, to be picked up by Bruce. Jim got the trash cow turned and drove it back to the herd. He located the last number four, in the middle of the huddled cattle. Copper pinned his ears as he galloped into the cows. He got the desired one against the fence, then turned it right and shoved it along the rail.

"Hyahh! Hyahh! Get movin'."

Jim drove that last cow as fast as it could run, with Copper right on its heels. Behind him, Bruce and Stoker were riding frantically back and forth across the ring, hats waving as they attempted to keep the rest of the nervous cows from stampeding over the foul line. The first cows Jim had cut out were standing in front of the pen's gate. Jim got them turned, and they ran into the pen, but his last cow attempted to run around the front of the pen and back to the herd. Copper put on a burst of speed, blocking the cow's path, sending it into its only avenue of escape, the pen. Jim pulled back hard on the reins, brought Copper to a sliding stop, then threw up his hand for time. Bruce and Stoker had bunched the rest of the cows back at the far end of the arena. A burst of applause came from the spectators. Bruce and Stoker left the cows and rode back to Jim's side.

Jim and his partners, sweat and dust covered

and breathing hard, as were their horses, waited tensely for their time. The murmuring from the crowd indicted they had a good run. The question was, was it good enough?

"What's takin' them so damn long?" Stoker said, as the minutes ticked by.

"Dunno," Jim said. "Copper came awful close to gettin' too far into the pen and disqualifyin' us, but I'm certain he stopped in time. Maybe they're just double-checking the time, or makin' certain none of our horses nipped a cow."

The P.A. system clicked to life.

"We have a new leader. Team thirteen, with a time of sixteen point six seconds. Sixteen point six. That means team thirteen, Rangers Jim Blawcyzk, Bruce Sherman, and Lieutenant Jameson Stoker will be the winners of this event, with an accumulated time for all three go-rounds of one minute, forty-five point four seconds. Their last run was one of the quickest, wildest team penning runs I've ever seen. Let's give them a big round of applause."

"Yeehaw!" Jim threw his hat in the air, jumped off Copper, hugged the horse's neck, then kissed him square on the nose. "I knew we could do it, boy. Extra grain for you tonight."

He didn't bother to remount, but led Copper out of the arena, with Bruce and Stoker trailing behind. Todd Lillis, Travis Benton, and John Drew were waiting for them.

"Jim, that was pure insanity in there, what you just pulled off. Congratulations," Lillis said. "That goes for all of you."

Now that the competition was over, except for the last few teams, who were too far behind to pass the leaders, the time for trash talk was over.

"Thanks, Todd. You didn't make it easy on us. Soon as we get the gear off our horses and have 'em cooled down, you want to grab a couple of beers? I'll buy. I can afford to now."

"Of course I'll have some beers," Lillis answered. "After all, you'll be payin' for 'em with my money."

"That's right," Jim said, laughing.

"Anything else I can do for you, Jim?" Lillis asked.

"Yeah. Figure out who's doing all the killings up in Llano County."

"I've been following that case," Lillis answered. "Let's do some brainstorming over our beers. Just maybe, I can come up with something."

"Appreciate that, Todd."

12

Bubba Abbott was at the high school baseball field, with a bucket of scuffed up baseballs at his feet. Although he was a pitcher, he was practicing his hitting, tossing a ball in the air, then swinging his bat and trying to drive the ball into the outfield. He stopped when he saw a familiar figure approaching.

"Hey, Bubba. I haven't seen you around town for a while," the man said, once he got near. "But I'd heard you were around, and I figured I'd find you here. What brings you back home?"

"We didn't make the playoffs, which means our season is over. I came home to visit my family, and see how the town's doin'," Abbott answered. "I was gonna look you up tomorrow, Dale. Good to see you again. What've you been up to?"

"Good to see you too. Not a helluva lot. Been doin' some odd jobs, besides workin' on my farm. Looks like you're gettin' some practice in. Want me to throw you a few pitches?"

"Sure, that'd be great. We can head over to Joe's Bar and Grille for a couple of cold ones after we're done, if that suits your fancy. Maybe there'll be a couple of gals we can sweet talk into spendin' the night with us."

"It certainly does. I'll grab my glove outta my truck. Be right back."

"C'mon, Laurie Jean. No one'll be around, I promise you."

"Are you sure, Robbie? I'd hate to be dis-covered."

"We're goin' to the high school field, in the middle of the summer, after dark. The lights won't be on, and there ain't gonna be anyone around to see us."

Laurie Jean Bohannon and Robbie Voos were both fifteen, smitten with each other, and in the throes of young love.

"I . . . I'm not certain this is right, Robbie."

"Of course it is. When two people are in love, it's what happens naturally."

"I just . . . don't want anyone else to know. And I want this to be special."

"It'll be our secret, just mine and yours. I want tonight to be special, too. And if it doesn't feel right, we can stop anytime. Does that make you feel better?"

"I . . . guess so. It's just, well . . ."

"I know, Laurie." Robbie kissed her gently on the lips. "Does that make it feel right?"

"Yes. Oh, Robbie, yes. I do love you."

"Good. Then let's get where no one will see us."

Robbie led her to the visitor's dugout. They

were halfway down the steps when Laurie Jean stiffened, then gasped. She pointed to an object on the dugout's floor.

"Robbie, what's that?"

"I don't know. Let me shine some light on it."

He took a Zippo cigarette lighter from his shirt pocket, and flicked it alight.

"What the hell?"

Laurie Jean began screaming uncontrollably at the sight of Bubba Abbott's body, blood pooling around the smashed skull.

13

Jim had decided to spend the week in Llano, hoping perhaps, if the murderer struck again, he'd be on scene fast enough to run him to ground. So far, he'd come up empty. This day had been a particularly frustrating one. He'd spent the morning re-questioning potential witnesses, but none could provide more information. The Hannaford-Smythes seemed to have left town. They'd checked out of the Dabbs, leaving no word with the clerk as to where they were headed.

While he was working on a plate of wings at Stonewall's Pizza, Wings and Things, the call he'd been waiting on from Austin had come through. The toxicology and DNA results on all four victims were complete, along with the DNA tests on the evidence Jim had collected. Jim asked the lab to email him the results at Stacy Hernandez's office, in the Llano County Sheriff's Office Complex. He went over the results himself, then called in Sheriff Avery, Deputy Kennedy, and Investigator Haskins.

"Did the tests turn up anything?" Avery asked, as he settled into a chair.

"Yeah, but not much more'n we already knew,

or had guessed," Jim answered. "I've made copies for all of you. You can go over them on your own. First, and most important, they confirm one and the same person committed all four murders. He's a white male with dark brown hair and brown eyes, probably in his early- to mid-twenties. His fingerprints were at all four scenes, along with traces of his DNA, except at the scene in Pontotoc. His prints were there, but no usable DNA. Nguyen's blood was on the scrap of cloth I found, along with the suspect's DNA. That definitely places him at one scene. The footprints from the llanite dike and by the river also match. The same gun was used in the ambushes on me and Lieutenant Stoker. It has to be our suspect that pulled the trigger."

"Sure doesn't narrow our profile down much, does it?" Kennedy said.

"No, it sure doesn't."

"Ranger, what about the toxicology reports?" Haskins asked.

"I'm comin' to those. As you know, Lillian Gates and Mary Connors were growin' and sellin' marijuana. No traces of any drugs were found in Gates's tissue or blood samples.

"The male victim in Pontotoc was indeed Hispanic, which means most likely Mexican. He was approximately fifty-five years old. He had heroin in his tissues. Due to the poor condition of the samples, and the elapsed time between the murder and the discovery of the body, the lab couldn't come up with a definite answer as to how much."

"So at least two of the victims were involved with drugs, either using or selling them," Avery said.

"That's right," Jim answered. "It gets even more interesting. Joe Benson had a trace of crack in his system. More significantly, samples from bags of his ground coffee didn't come back as plain old java."

"Weed?" Kennedy asked.

"And crack. Apparently, Benson's business wasn't making all the money from lattes and espressos."

"That crack'd give a body a whole lot better jolt than plain old caffeine," Avery said.

"And the weed would help a dude mellow out, and also give him a case of the munchies," Haskins added. "No wonder Joe sold so many candy bars and cupcakes."

"How about Nguyen?" Avery asked.

"There were traces of marijuana in his system."

"That means all four were either dealing, or using, drugs," Kennedy said.

"Correct. However, that doesn't necessarily mean drugs are the connection between all the victims. It's a good possibility, but we don't have enough evidence to prove it."

"Plus, there's the chickens," Avery said.

"Yep, there's the chickens, and one duck. Why is the suspect killing birds in the same manner as his human victims, then leaving the carcasses with the corpses? It's sure a puzzlement."

"So, where do we go from here, Jim?" Avery asked.

"Just keep doin' more legwork. See if we can come up with someone who saw something. See if anyone might've known that Mexican, and just doesn't want to talk. Keep Webb and Sloan under observation. Keep an eye out for the English couple, in case they turn up in town again. Fred, have Deputy Lamoureux keep pluggin' away in Kingsland. Maybe the paper'll receive another message. Try'n find some reason why the victims were chosen. I'm convinced they weren't picked at random."

"Well, we'd best get on it," Avery said. "Boys, let's take our copies and see if we find somethin' in those reports. Jim, what're you gonna do for the rest of the day?"

"Go through all the evidence yet again. There's *got* to be somethin' I missed."

"Then, we'll leave you to it."

About four that afternoon, Jim closed the case folder on the Gates murder, and leaned back in his chair.

"Damn! I'm getting nowhere. It's still hot as

blazes outside, and the a/c's just about given up in here. I'm gonna call it a day and cool off. Reckon I'll head for the river. Maybe I'll go tubin'. It's high time I cleared my head."

14

Jim rented two tubes, one for himself, the other to hold his cooler and a six-pack of Dr Pepper. His cell phone and pistol were in a waterproof sack, which hung from a lanyard around his neck, and rested on his chest. He put the tubes into the Llano River at Badu Park.

Since the Llano was dammed to form a lake, just above the historic steel bridge which carried Texas 16 over the river, the current was slow and lazy, just what Jim was looking for. He spent the next three hours lazing in the river, enjoying the hot sun and cool water as he floated along, occasionally paddling a bit upstream, or out into deeper, cooler water. For the first hour, he wracked his brain in a futile attempt to come up with a motive for the string of murders or recall something in the backgrounds of the victims that might connect one to their murderer. He gave it up as a bad effort and forced himself to clear his mind of all thoughts but the calming effects of the river. With his old Stetson pulled low over his face, he even dozed off a time or two.

When the sun neared the western horizon, and the breeze carried an evening chill, Jim got out of the river. He used a stall in the men's room to change from his swim trunks into jeans and a

T-shirt. He buckled his gunbelt around his waist and replaced his sweat-stained old Stetson on his head. He drove up Birmingham Avenue, past Laura Webb's house, where there was no sign of anyone home.

Famished, Jim turned onto West Young Street searching for a restaurant. When he saw a banner at the edge of the road for an All You Can Eat Buffet, he pulled into the lot of the Llano's Hungry Hunter restaurant.

"Lot's full of pickups, and something sure smells good. I reckon this is the place," he said to himself, as he got out of the Tahoe.

The restaurant offered far more than promised on the banner. The buffet was overflowing with a great variety, from soups and salads to main course and desserts. Jim sampled several of the more tempting items, taking his time and enjoying the meal. He'd just finished a piece of coconut cream pie when his phone rang.

"Ranger Blawcyzk."

"Jim, it's Fred. We have another one."

"Another one? Where?"

"At the baseball field behind the high school. That's off 16, just past the junction with 71 East. You'll need to use the second entrance."

"I'll be there in three minutes."

Jim gulped down the last of his coffee, threw some bills on the table to pay for his meal, ran to his truck, and switched on the lights and siren.

He roared out of the lot, rubber squealing and tires smoking.

Once again, Jim rolled up to a scene of emergency vehicles, flood lights, and curious spectators standing behind the ubiquitous yellow crime scene tape. He pulled up to the deputy blocking the road and lowered his window.

"The sheriff's waitin' for you in front of the visitor's dugout, Ranger."

"*Gracias.*"

Sheriff Avery waved Jim down when he reached the edge of the field.

"What've you got, Fred?"

"One male victim, and one helluva mess."

"What d'ya mean by that?"

"You'll see, soon as you take a look."

"Just let me grab my evidence kit. Give me some more details."

"It's the same killer, all right. Dead man is Luther "Bubba" Abbott. He was a star pitcher in high school. Real popular with the girls, too, good-lookin' kid, tall, blond hair, light blue eyes. A real All-American type. He got a baseball scholarship to Texas A & M. Once he graduated, he got a spot on a semi-pro league team, over to Georgetown. From what I understand, he just signed on with the Astros, and was assigned to their Double A club. I wasn't aware he had come back home. A couple of teenagers found the body."

Jim gestured to a young couple sitting inside a Llano Police Department vehicle, along with Jody Kennedy.

"Those the ones?"

"Yeah. They're both too upset to get anything out of 'em. It's pretty obvious they were comin' here for a make-out session. They did tell us they didn't see anyone around the field."

"You said the victim is white?"

"White as white bread."

"Which means, unless we turn up something in his background, we can pretty much eliminate hate as a motive."

"Let's see what we've got."

Jim entered the dugout. Abbott's body was lying face-up in the far corner. Blood, still only partially dried, spread around his head. In the center of the puddle was a baseball. More blood darkened the crotch of his jeans, and the lower half of his polo shirt. Alongside Abbott's remains was the bloody carcass of a rooster. Abbott's glove was still on his left hand, his bat still gripped in his right.

"I see what you mean by a helluva mess, Fred. Let me get to work."

Jim took photos of the body, several samples of the blood, then began his examination of the corpse. He rolled Abbott's body onto its right hip and removed the wallet from its left hip pocket. He took out the driver's license.

"Victim is Luther Abbott, age 23. Address on license is 25 Water's Edge Circle, Apartment 22, Georgetown. His identity has been confirmed by Llano County Sheriff Frederick Avery.

"Victim has been dead for less than approximately two to three hours. Rigor mortis has just begun, and few signs of livor mortis are present. There is a severe injury to the victim's forehead, a depression indicating a probable skull fracture. A baseball next to the victim's head is the possible instrument which caused the wound. That will be confirmed upon forensics testing. The right side of the victim's skull has also been crushed. There is a baseball bat, its barrel blood-soaked, gripped in the victim's right hand.

"A preliminary indication would be the victim was killed by a blow from that bat, which was then placed in his hand. Again, that will be confirmed by forensics tests. Pending a complete autopsy and toxicology report, death was apparently caused by blunt force trauma."

Jim paused, then opened the unzipped fly of Abbott's jeans a bit wider. "Victim has been castrated, probably after being killed. Genitals are not with the body. Further search of the scene may locate them. I am now going to search the victim for any possible evidence."

Jim reached into Abbott's right front pants pocket, which held a set of keys, one for a Nissan, the other apparently a house key. Jim slid those into a baggie, then searched the left pocket. He removed a business card.

"What've you got, Jim?" Avery asked.

"The Snow Chicken Café, Austin. Seems like your All-American boy might've been there, maybe more'n once."

"That a restaurant? Is snow chicken some kind of specialty dish they serve?"

"Not exactly. It's a club. The 'snow' doesn't refer to the kind that falls from the sky. It's the kind you snort through a straw and up your nose."

"Cocaine?"

"Bingo. Seems like I'll have to make a trip to Austin tomorrow."

"I doubt anyone connected with the place will cooperate."

"Oh, they will," Jim said. "The owner will squawk a bit, pardon the pun, but he'll cooperate."

"You could let my people take over here, and go down there right now," Avery suggested. "The place must stay open late."

"I could, but the place is only open from Thursday through Sunday. Besides, and this is no reflection on your department, or the Llano P.D., but I can't chance someone sayin' the chain of custody for any evidence was broken. Some smart lawyer'd do just that, and just maybe convince a jury we didn't build a solid case."

"Understood, Jim. No offense taken."

"*Gracias*. Now, let's see what else we have."

Jim searched through the rest of Abbott's pockets, finding nothing of interest.

"Let me see if Abbott had anything in this glove."

Avery watched as Jim spread open the baseball glove on Abbott's left hand.

"What the hell are those?" Avery exclaimed, on seeing the contents.

"Those, Fred, are 'fowl balls'," Jim answered. "Which means that rooster is now a capon."

15

The Snow Chicken Café was located in a nondescript, white cinder block building in a small industrial area, which bordered one of Austin's trendiest districts. The only thing that distinguished it from any of the other buildings on the street was an eight-foot-tall fiberglass statue of a snow-white chicken, outside the front entrance. The caricature was dressed in a bikini, and had oversized breasts. A vinyl sign hanging on the wall behind the chicken proclaimed it was "Retro Disco Night." As usual, there was a line of patrons waiting to be admitted to the crowded club. With no parking for blocks, Jim pulled into the club's driveway, and left his truck there.

"Mister, you can't just leave that thing there," one of the bouncers shouted.

Jim pointed to his badge.

"This says I can. Make certain no one touches my vehicle now, y'all hear? I'd be plumb upset if someone did."

Leaving the bouncer staring gape-mouthed at his back, Jim walked past the line of patrons. The bouncer at the door put his hand on Jim's chest.

"Ranger, I don't know who you think you are, but you can't go in there."

Jim's blue eyes glittered like chips of ice.

"Who says I can't?"

"Me."

"Well, Mister Me, I can, and I will. Now, kindly remove your hand from my chest, before I remove it from your arm, permanently."

The bouncer started to frame a retort, then thought better of it.

"All right, Ranger. Go on in."

"Much obliged."

The dance floor was thronged with couples dancing to the Rod Stewart classic *Do Ya Think I'm Sexy?* Jim shoved his way through the mob and up to the bar.

"You look kinda out of place in here, Ranger," the nearest bartender said. "What the hell dropped you at my door?"

"I need to talk with Reilly. He in?"

"No one talks to Mr. Reilly without an appointment."

"He'll talk to me. Trust me on that."

"Maybe, but he's not here. He's in his office next door."

Jim tossed a twenty-dollar bill on the bar.

"Thanks. I'm obliged."

"Don't make this a habit, Ranger."

"Don't plan to."

Jim walked to the adjacent building, one nearly identical to the first, except this one was painted a deep gray. In front of its entrance stood another eight-foot-tall statue of a chicken, this one without any breasts, dressed only in a male's thong swimsuit. The sign above gave the club's name as the "Neuter Rooster." It catered to a gay clientele.

At the next door, Jim had to pass a line of patrons waiting to get inside, then fight his way through the mobbed dance floor. Tina Turner's *Better Be Good to Me* was blasting at full volume from the sound system.

"Nice outfit, cowboy, but you're two nights early," one of the dancers said. "Tonight's Pirate Night. Cowboy Night is Saturday."

"I'll keep that in mind," Jim answered, with a chuckle. He continued past the bar, to a door marked "Private", which was guarded by a burly security person.

"You lookin' for somethin'?" he asked.

"Yeah. John Reilly. Tell him Jim Blawcyzk needs to see him."

"I'll let him know, but he probably won't want to see *you*."

The man emphasized the last word, then disappeared behind the door. He returned a moment later with an astonished expression on his face.

"Mr. Reilly says come right in. You know which is his office, right?"

"I sure do."

Jim walked down a narrow hallway to the last

office on the right. John Reilly, owner of both clubs, was seated with his feet up on his desk, smoking a long cigar.

"Ranger Jim Blawcyzk. I'd like to say it's good to see you, but it isn't."

"Oh, I'd say it is. If it weren't for me, and your value to the law enforcement community, you'd have been shut down and behind bars a long time ago, John. You should welcome me with open arms. Besides, this won't take long."

"Suits me just fine. What do you want?"

"Have you been following the news about the killings up in Llano County?"

"Yeah, sure. What's that got to do with me?"

"There's been another one."

Jim took a copy of Bubba Abbott's college yearbook photograph from his shirt pocket and slid it across Reilly's desk.

"Do you happen to recognize this *hombre*?"

"Why, should I?"

"He's the latest victim. He had a card from the Snow Chicken in his pocket when his body was found."

"So? Why should I recognize him? I get lots of his kind at my places."

"What do you mean, 'his kind'?"

"Young, good-looking guys, who want to score with the chicks. They all start to look the same after a while."

"Don't play games with me. Take a closer look.

Unless you'd prefer a visit from Austin P.D.'s narcotics squad."

"All right, I've seen the kid around here, quite a bit. What's his name?"

"Luther Abbott, goes by Bubba. I'm bettin' you already knew that. Baseball player, just signed on with the Astros. He was supposed to start with their Double A club. Instead, he's dead. Interesting part is whoever killed him castrated him, kinda like that poor big ol' rooster you've got standing out front. So, can you tell me anything about him?"

"Not really. He was just another guy looking for some action."

"How about friends. Anyone come with him, regularly?"

"Now that you mention it, yeah. Odd duck."

"You got a name?"

"Lemme think. Yeah, Dale. Dale Fulton."

"What'd this Fulton look like?"

"Pretty much the opposite of Abbott. Abbott was always well-dressed, with not a hair out of place. Fulton has long, dark hair, and a scraggly beard. Usually showed up in overalls and a T-shirt. Kind of a hardscrabble farmer type. Talked a lot about being a vegetarian, animal rights, and all that nonsense. Only reason he was allowed in was him being friends with Abbott. Plus, he never gave the help a hard time, and he tipped them real well. Never could figure out him and Abbott bein' buds. They were an odd couple if ever I saw one."

"You wouldn't, by chance, happen to know where this Fulton lives?"

"I sure don't, but I got the impression he and Abbott came from the same town. That's about all I can tell you."

"John, as usual, you've been a great help. Appreciate the information."

"Don't spread that around, Blawcyzk. Word like that gets out on the streets, it could ruin my business."

"We sure wouldn't want that to happen, would we? Certainly not to a fine, upstanding member of the community such as yourself. Don't get up. I'll see myself out. If you think of anything else, you know how to reach me."

"Sadly, I sure do, you bastard."

"Uh-uh. Like Tina was just singin' when I came in, Reilly. If you know what's good for you, you'd better be good to me."

Once he was back on the road, Jim dialed Deputy Kennedy's number.

"Jody, it's Jim. Do you happen to know an *hombre* name of Dale Fulton?"

"Hey, I was just gonna call you. Bonnie Tyson from the *News* got another note from our suspect. It was left under her windshield wiper."

"What'd this one say?"

266

"Those who kill the innocent will die."

"They're gettin' more threatening with each one. Now, can you tell me anything about Dale Fulton?"

"Oh, sure. He's kind of the county eccentric. Always carrying on about what we're doing to the planet, that mankind is doomed, all that stuff. He drives an old Army six by six truck. He mounted a pickup camper to its bed. Even weirder, he's got a chicken coop under the camper. Wherever he goes, those birds go. He's a strange *hombre*, but he's never bothered anyone."

"You happen to know where he lives?"

"Yup. He took over a couple of the old shacks in Click. Been squattin' there ever since he got out of high school. That's a ghost town, about twenty miles southeast of Llano. Why do you ask?"

"Because I've just found out he and Bubba Abbott were friends. They hung out at the Snow Chicken in Austin."

"Drugs?"

"I don't know for certain, but I'd say Fulton is a person of interest, in at least one murder. Maybe all of them."

"You want me to pick him up?"

"Not yet. I'm about an hour from Click. Head that way, and I'll meet you there. Just observe his place until I arrive. I don't want you goin' in there without backup. If Fulton does make a move, then stop him. But only if. Let your office know what we're doing."

"Will do. I'll meet you at the intersection of 308 and 3088."

"Okay, but you be careful. If Fulton is our man, he's mighty dangerous."

"I'm a cautious son of a bitch. No need to worry about me. See you in Click."

"See you there."

16

The night was hot and sticky, so Kennedy had his windows down while he watched the tumble-down shack Dale Fulton called home. Fulton's old Army six by was parked alongside it. The terrain here was level, the vegetation sparse, so Kennedy was parked far enough away he could use his binoculars to spy on Fulton, but where, in the dark, it would be highly unlikely Fulton would discover his presence.

He'd been on scene about twenty minutes, when he saw a light flare inside one of Fulton's outbuildings. A moment later, the hair-raising scream of a human in extreme pain shattered the still night. Kennedy reacted instantly, speeding down the rutted track that had once been Click's Main Street. Gun in hand, he leapt out of his car, then kicked open the building's door. The sight which confronted him was so gruesome he stopped in his tracks, his guts churning and bile rising in his throat. Before he could recover from his shock, Dale Fulton was on him. He kicked Fulton in the groin, doubling him to the ground in agony. Fulton grabbed a rifle leaning against the wall and put two bullets into the deputy's back. Satisfied Kennedy was dead, he turned back to the task at hand.

• • •

Half-an-hour later, Jim arrived at the meeting spot.

"Where in the hell is Jody?" he muttered. "I hope nothing's gone wrong."

He drove a bit farther past the junction, to the dirt track which led to the ruins of Click. Two sets of tire tracks went in, but only one, from a heavy truck, came out.

"That's Jody's car down there. I'll bet he's in trouble."

Jim sped down the road, his Tahoe jouncing wildly as he ignored the chuckholes and ruts. He skidded to a stop, dust swirling, half expecting a hail of bullets to riddle the Tahoe and cut him down. He got out of the truck, pulled his Ruger from its holster, and approached the only building which showed light inside.

"Texas Ranger!" He repeated, "Texas Ranger!" When there was no response, he opened the door, staying to one side.

The scene inside hit him like a kick in the gut. Though he was used to investigating the most ghastly of crimes, Jim nearly dropped to his knees, nausea grabbing at his insides. A man lay dismembered on the dirt floor. He had a rope burn around his neck, had been disemboweled, and then torn into four pieces, his arms and legs ripped from their sockets. Just inside the door lay Jody Kennedy, face down, with two bullet holes

270

in his back. Jim slid his gun back in its holster and rolled the deputy onto his back. Kennedy had two exit holes in his chest, but somehow still held onto a spark of life.

"Jody, can you hear me? It's Jim. Jim Blawcyzk."

Kennedy's eyes fluttered open.

"Jim?"

"Yeah. Hold on. I'm gonna try'n reach Dispatch, and get you some help."

Jim dialed the number, praying that he'd have cell service in this remote spot. He gave a sigh of relief when he heard the phone at the other end ring.

"Llano County Dispatch, what's your emergency?"

"Dispatch, this is Ranger Unit 810. I have an officer down, shot and badly wounded. Need a medical chopper here *now*. Location is the ghost town of Click, off 308 and 3088.

"10-4, Ranger. Will order chopper immediately."

"I'll stay on the line. Soon as you summon that chopper, I need to put out an A.P.B."

"Right, Ranger."

"Help's on the way, Jody," he reassured the deputy, while he waited for the dispatcher to come back on the line. "Don't you quit on me."

"Chopper is en route. ETA thirty minutes."

"Good. I need Sheriff Avery notified I need him here ASAP. Along with the county coroner, and two or three deputies. Also need all law authorities within Llano County, and the adjacent counties, to be on the lookout for a converted six by six Army truck. Vehicle has camper and chicken coop on top. Probably still painted in camouflage, with Texas plates. Driver will be Dale Fulton, early twenties, long brown hair and beard. Suspected in Llano County murders. Subject is armed and extremely dangerous."

"An Army truck with a camper and chicken coop?"

"That's correct."

"10-4. Just confirming I heard you correctly."

"You did. Ranger 810, out."

"Dispatch, out."

"Be right back, Jody."

Jim went to his truck and got his first aid kit, then knelt at the deputy's side.

"You hang in there, buddy. I'm gonna patch you up until the EMTs arrive. Shouldn't take 'em too long."

"Sorry this happened . . . Jim. I was watchin' the place, like you . . . said. Heard a man scream like . . . like he'd just come face . . . to face with . . . the devil himself. Had to . . ."

"No need to explain. You did what needed doin'. Just save your strength. As far as that poor *hombre* lyin' over there, I do believe he had the misfortune of crossing Satan right here on earth. You did, too."

"Shouldn't have let him . . . get jump . . . on me. When I saw . . . that . . ."

"No need to say more. I'm still feeling a bit queasy myself at that sight. I've never seen a man hung, drawn, and quartered in my life, and I pray to God I never see one again. Now, keep quiet so I can try'n get this bleedin' stopped."

Jim cut off Kennedy's shirt, put stacks of gauze bandages on the holes in his chest, taped them in place, then rolled him onto his stomach. He placed more gauze over the wounds in Kennedy's back, taped those in place, then used a long strip of cloth to put pressure on the wounds, wrapping it around the deputy as tightly as possible, tied it off, then rolled Kennedy onto his back once again. Lastly, he covered the deputy with a blanket, then raised his feet, using an old beam to support them. If Kennedy went into shock, he would lose his fight for life.

"Jody, I've done everything I can for you. Sheriff Avery's on the way, along with the medevac. You mind if I start processing the scene while we're waiting?"

"No, go ahead."

"One quick question. Was it Dale Fulton who shot you?"

"The damn bastard . . . sure did. If I . . . pull through, he'll regret it."

After putting on his protective clothing, Jim began taking photographs of the scene. When he finished, he gathered what evidence he could find. Not being able to delay any longer, he went through the dead man's pockets. He removed the man's wallet and took out his driver's license.

"Morton Gould, 54 years old, from Buchanan Dam," he read.

"Jim, I'm feelin' really weak," Kennedy said. "Reckon I'm not . . . gonna make it."

"I'm not lettin' you quit on me now, Deputy. I'll need your testimony to nail the son of a bitch who shot you to the wall. The medics will be here in less than fifteen minutes. Don't try'n talk anymore. Conserve your strength."

"All right, Rang . . ." Kennedy drifted into unconsciousness.

Jim continued examining the dismembered body until he heard an approaching car, its siren blaring. He stepped outside to intercept Sheriff Avery before he could enter the shack. Avery slammed his Suburban into park before the vehicle even stopped rolling, the gears grinding in protest. The sheriff jumped out before it had come to a complete stop.

"Jim, what the hell happened?"

"Let me explain a little of that before I let you inside, Fred. I got a good lead from the Snow Chicken's owner. He gave me a name, Dale Fulton. Jody Kennedy knew Fulton, and where he lived. I asked Jody to keep an eye on Fulton until I got here. Jody heard a scream, decided he couldn't wait, and walked in on Fulton killin' a man. The son of a bitch shot Jody in the back, twice. I don't know how, but Jody's still hangin' on. Before I let you inside, I've got to warn you, it's really nasty inside that shack. Even turned my stomach."

"I'm not worried about that. I just want to see Jody."

"Of course you do. Let's go."

Jim led Avery into the shack. The sheriff's gaze was involuntarily drawn to the torn apart corpse. He gasped, and grabbed at his stomach.

"I warned you, Fred. Don't look at it. Jody's unconscious, but talk to him until the chopper arrives. Should be any minute."

"Sure. Sure, Jim. What the hell happened to that poor devil?"

"Offhand, it appears Fulton knew the ancient British manner of torturing a prisoner to death: hanging, drawing, and quartering. The condemned person was hung, but not until dead, then disemboweled, while still alive. Finally, his arms and legs were shackled, either to a winch, or by ropes to four horses, and he was literally torn into four pieces. Sometimes, the man was simply chopped into four pieces. Looks like that was done here."

"Oh, my Lord. We're dealing with a monster!"

"To put it mildly. Listen. The chopper's coming. You stay with Jody while I signal them."

"Okay."

Jim turned on his truck's headlights to indicate a landing place for the helicopter. The paramedics grabbed their gear and followed Jim into the shack. They gave Gould's corpse a glance, then went over to where Jody lay, pale as death, his breathing hardly noticeable.

"He still alive?" one asked Avery.

"Barely. Do the best you can for him."

"We'll try everything we can to save him."

"Fred, do you want to head for the hospital?" Jim asked.

"No. The best way for me to help Jody is by helping track down the *hombre* who did this."

"He shouldn't be too hard to find. He's driving an old Army six by with a camper and chicken coop. That thing'll stick out like those English folks did in Llano."

"You said this murder was done with an old English method of execution. You think those people might've been involved somehow?"

"The thought had crossed my mind, but the only tire tracks I found belonged to Jody's car, and a heavy truck. If they are involved, they must have paid Fulton to do their dirty work. My gut tells me Fulton was working alone."

Once the paramedics had Jody stabilized, they put him on a stretcher and carried him to the helicopter, strapping him in place.

"We'll have him at Ascension Seton Southwest

in twenty minutes," the pilot said. "There's a trauma team already on standby. Your deputy will get the best possible care, Sheriff."

"*Gracias*," Avery said. He and Jim watched the chopper lift off, then head toward Austin. It had no sooner risen over the county road when a series of shots rang out, aimed at the machine. Sparks flew from one of its landing runners when a bullet struck it, then ricocheted into the dark. The chopper rose quickly when the pilot shoved the control stick fully forward. It turned sharply left and right in an evasive maneuver, then straight toward Austin.

"That bastard was lyin' in wait, and now he's tryin' to shoot down the chopper!" Avery exclaimed.

"I think he was waitin' to get us," Jim said. "He must've thought Jody was already dead, or he would have finished him off. Let's get him."

When Jim opened the Tahoe's door, a bullet punched through it. Another one hit the lower right-hand corner of the windshield, spider-webbing most of the right half.

"I'm not gonna be as easy to kill as the others, damn you," Jim muttered. He threw the Tahoe into gear and jammed the accelerator to the floor.

17

It didn't take long for Jim to catch up with the lumbering Army truck. While the heavy vehicle was no match for Jim's Tahoe's speed, it was impossible for him to get around it, and ramming it would be an exercise in futility. Jim, with Avery right behind him, kept on the truck's tail as the driver continued north on 308, evidently heading for Llano. He keyed his radio's mic.

"Dispatch, Ranger 810."

"Ranger 810, Dispatch. Go ahead."

"In pursuit of suspect's vehicle, northbound on County 308. Need roadblock at 308 and Texas 71. Notify Llano County, also Llano Police. Leave this channel open."

"10-4, Ranger 810."

As Jim had expected, Fulton reached the junction with Texas 71 before a roadblock could be set in place. Fulton turned west on 71, heading for downtown Llano. Jim keyed his mic again.

"Ranger 810 to Dispatch."

"Go ahead, Ranger 810."

"Suspect's vehicle has already passed intersection with 71. New location for roadblocks would be 71 and Texas 16. Also need one at the south end of the 16 bridge over the river."

"10-4, Ranger 810. Will advise."

When they approached the intersection of 71 and 16, Jim could see two Llano Police Ford Tauruses, nose-to-nose, completely blocking the road. The police officers standing next to them emptied their pistols at Fulton's truck, but were forced to dive out of the way when Fulton's six by smashed through the barrier.

"Dispatch, he got past the first roadblock," Jim spoke into his mic. "Now heading for the bridge."

"This is Llano County 93. I'll stop him."

Jim recognized the voice as belonging to Deputy Claire Lamoureux. He uttered a silent prayer she would be able to stop Fulton before anyone else got hurt, or worse. He heard the blast of a shotgun over his mic, then Fulton's truck swerved violently to the right.

"Got him!" Jim heard Lamoureux exclaim.

Fulton's truck went off the road into Grenwelge Park, which was a rough, rock outcropping strewn parcel along the Llano. It crashed through the restroom building, then crossed East Haynie Street and came to a stop against the old Llano Red Top jail, now being preserved as a museum. Fulton jumped out of his vehicle, rolled, took several shots at his pursuers, then dove through a window, shattering the glass, and into the jail. Jim stopped behind Fulton's truck, blocking it in.

"Everybody, stay back," he ordered.

"Fred, I want this building surrounded. I'm goin' in there alone."

"Alone? That's crazy."

"No, it's not. That jail is a maze inside. If a whole bunch of us go in there, we're liable to end up shootin' one of our own people. You seal this perimeter tight as an unopened jar of salsa. Don't come in, even if you hear shots, until I tell you to. Or if the shots stop, and I don't give the all clear, then come in."

"It's your ball game, Jim."

Jim switched on his truck's P.A.

"Dale Fulton. This is the Texas Rangers! We have the jail surrounded. You have no way out. Give yourself up."

"Go to hell, Ranger!"

Fulton answered with a volley of rifle fire.

"Then I'm comin' in," Jim answered. Knowing it would be a close-quarters fight, he left his rifle on the hood of his Tahoe and removed his Ruger from its holster. He crept alongside the jail's wall and climbed through the same window Fulton had used.

Fulton was not in any of the first-floor offices when Jim searched them. When he climbed the stairs to the second, several shots rang out, ricocheting wildly off the metal stairs and bannisters. Jim returned two shots, just to drive Fulton back.

The cells were enveloped in almost complete darkness. The only light came from a nearby streetlamp, and the flashes of the guns. Jim caught a glimpse of Fulton running in front of an open cell, and took a snap shot. He was rewarded with a cry of pain. Fulton sagged against the bars. When Jim drew nearer, Fulton grabbed a chicken from inside the cell. He threw the squawking bird into Jim's face, then kicked him in the belly, shoved him in the cell, and slammed the door shut, locking it.

"I reckon I win, Ranger," he snarled. "You can sit there a while and think about dyin'."

"Not today," Jim shot back. Fulton had neglected to take his gun. Jim shot him in the hip. Fulton crumpled. Jim then shot the lock, opening the door.

"Sheriff, it's all clear. I've got him."

To Fulton he said, "I guess Chicken Little was right. The sky really was falling . . . for you."

18

Jim was conducting a post-mortem with Lieutenant Stoker, Sheriff Avery, and Investigator Haskins. Jody Kennedy faced a long recovery, but would survive.

"I still can't believe that place where Fulton lived," Haskins said.

"Yeah, but after retrieving his Browning BLR, and all the other evidence, there's no doubt he'll be found guilty, and executed," Jim said.

"And we saved a lot more lives," Avery noted. "Those drawings on the walls at Fulton's place were just demented."

"Yeah," Jim agreed. "A sketch of putting a person and pheasant under glass, and one of barbequing a bird and a person on a rotisserie. Then the drawing of what he wanted to do to the Hannaford-Smythes."

"You'd better explain that," Stoker said.

"It's an Italian dish, chicken cacciatore. Since the Hannaford-Smythes were from England, and British loyalists during the American Revolution were called Tories, he was going to prepare Chicken Catch a Tory. Luckily, they left for Waco before he got to them."

"Time for some leave, Ranger," Stoker said.

"Not until he explains Fulton's motive again," Avery said.

"He was insane. He was upset about people killing fowl for food. So, he was goin' after anyone involved with selling poultry products. Lillian Gates sold organic chicken. The Mexican feller, whom I guess we'll never identify, must've been involved in cock-fighting. Joe Benson managed a Perfect Chick before he opened his coffee shop. Nguyen Tranh sold plenty of chicken to restaurants, especially General Tso's chicken. And Morton Gould owned a factory egg farm. Bubba Abbott played for the Georgetown Prairie Hens. But we were lucky to stop Fulton when we did. He had plans to fill his truck with explosives and blow up the big Lone Star Chicken place over to Tyler."

"But why did he kill those birds?"

"In his twisted logic, he thought he was making his reasons clear."

"We can finish this discussion later," Stoker said. "It's time to call it a day."

"I won't argue with you about that," Jim answered.

19

"I don't understand what you're doing," Jim said to Kim and Betty. Why are you blindfolding me, and taking me to the Howfields'?"

"You'll see in a minute," Kim said.

They walked Jim into the Howfields' backyard.

"Now you can take off the blindfold," Kim said.

Jim opened his eyes to see a 1989 Chevrolet Caprice station wagon, fully restored as a Texas Ranger vehicle of the era.

"Happy Birthday!" everyone shouted.

"This-this is mine?" Jim stammered.

"It sure is," Porter said. "We had to work hard to keep it a secret from you."

"And here's our other secret," Babs said. "We're going to build a barn. We're getting horses, adopting two dogs and three cats, and getting some chickens and ducks."

"That's great," Jim said. "Looks like I win the bet, Kim. And thank all of you. I'm overwhelmed."

"Our lunch is just about ready," Babs said.

"What are we having?" Jim asked.

"Barbequed chicken."

"Oh, no!" Jim groaned, then burst into laughter

About the Author

Jim Griffin became enamored of the Texas Rangers from watching the TV series, Tales of the Texas Rangers, as a youngster. He grew to be an avid student and collector of Rangers' artifacts, memorabilia, and other items. His collection is now housed in the Texas Ranger Hall of Fame and Museum in Waco.

His quest for authenticity in his writing has taken him to the famous Old West towns of Pecos, Deadwood, Cheyenne, Tombstone and numerous others. While Jim's books are fiction, he strives to keep them as accurate as possible within the realm of fiction.

A graduate of Southern Connecticut State University, Jim now lives in Keene, New Hampshire when he isn't traveling around the west.

A devoted and enthusiastic horseman, Jim bought his first horse when he was a junior in college. He has owned several American Paint horses. He is a member of the Connecticut Horse Council Volunteer Horse Patrol, an organization which assists the state park Rangers with patrolling parks and forests.

Jim's books are highly reminiscent of the pulp westerns of yesteryear—the heroes and villains are clearly separated.

Website: www.jamesjgriffin.net

Books are produced in the United States using U.S.-based materials

Books are printed using a revolutionary new process called THINKtech™ that lowers energy usage by 70% and increases overall quality

Books are durable and flexible because of Smyth-sewing

Paper is sourced using environmentally responsible foresting methods and the paper is acid-free

Center Point Large Print
600 Brooks Road / PO Box 1
Thorndike, ME 04986-0001 USA

(207) 568-3717

US & Canada:
1 800 929-9108
www.centerpointlargeprint.com